Praise for *The Return of the Century*

"Sparkling storytelling, colorful cast of characters, and a voyage of discovery: if you love Oscar Wilde you will love this book."
—Marilyn Bisch and Joan Navarre, co-founders of The Oscar Wilde Society of America

"Reading and reading again *The Return of the Century* I was fascinated. Oscar Wilde is not only a contemporary icon but a state of mind that regenerates itself by revealing, still today, unpublished episodes, anecdotes, characters. This book by Ardythe Ashley is a treasure chest!"
—Renato Miracco, art historian, critic, and author of *Oscar Wilde's Italian Dream 1875–1900*

"Like the sensual kisses that encompass Oscar Wilde's tomb, Ardythe Ashley has breathed life into the erotic poetics of Wilde's literary and biographical life. Ashley's writing makes you want to travel to Paris so you can walk along the Seine with Oscar and all of the men in his life. After reading her novel, you might even see Oscar beckoning you to enter into his romantic rendezvous."
—Andrew Rimby, Executive Director of the podcast *The Ivory Tower Boiler Room*

"There are two resurrections in history. One ended in heaven, the other in Paris and Venice. In a titanic effort, Ardythe Ashley brings Oscar Wilde back to life. It is the return of the century!"
—Nikolai Endres, Western Kentucky University

THE RETURN OF THE CENTURY

First Warbler Press Edition 2022

The Return of the Century: The Death and Further Adventures of Oscar Wilde
© Ardythe Ashley 2022

An earlier version of this book was published as *The Reflections of Narcissus: The Death and Further Adventures of Oscar Wilde* in 2012

ISBN 978-1-957240-18-3 (paperback)
ISBN 978-1-957240-19-0 (e-book)

warblerpress.com

THE RETURN OF THE CENTURY

THE DEATH AND FURTHER ADVENTURES OF OSCAR WILDE

ARDYTHE ASHLEY

warbler press

DEDICATION

To Rob and Maurice, two pillars of friendship,
without whom New York City is not New York City.

"Most people are other people..."

—Oscar Wilde
De Profundis

CONTENTS

PREFACE

If you are looking for Oscar Wilde you can visit his famous grave in the Père Lachaise Cemetery of Paris. There you will see his name carved into stone. But if you seek the living Oscar Wilde you can find him in one place only.

It is essential that you go at night. The moon must be visible, preferably full, and the air, temperate. You must go alone. Begin in the sixth *arrondissement* of Paris where Oscar lived out his final days of exile. Make your way through the narrow streets to the wooden footbridge that allows you to traverse the River Seine from the magnificent dome of the Académie des Beaux-Arts to the portals of the Louvre. (The French love their symbolism.) A short distance out from the left bank, perhaps one hundred paces, you stop and lean against the western railing, facing in the direction of the Eiffel Tower. Be sure no one loiters nearby. Stand very still. Let the night enter into you.

From where you are now positioned look straight down into the dark waters of the flowing river, then lift your eyes slightly, across the watery expanse, to the lower quays along the right bank where lovers meet in sprays of lamp light the color of yellow wine. In the darker spaces between the street lamps, you see the spark of matches laid to the ends of cigarettes. You know they belong to the street boys who wait there. You feel yourself grow large in stature as you watch these small worlds of love and their loveless imitations. You light a cigarette from your own meager supply. You ponder the boys and think if you will go down amongst them. Some of them, you know, will be beautiful. No. Tonight you are merely an observer. Your eyes narrow as you look up from the distant quays, quietly reveling in the sensations that visit upon you—the sound of moving water, the outline of Paris against the glow of night, the mingling of smoke and air in your lungs.

Prudence says that it is late and that you must be going, but here in the midst of so much beauty you are unready to return to your narrow bed. The bed upon which you know you soon must die. You feel both the profound sadness at what has happened to you, what will happen to you, and an unexpected exaltation in the present moment. It is a sublime confection.

The moonlight absorbs you, keeps you still, and you know that some part of you will remain here, in this place, standing upon this bridge, keeping a silent vigil as the decades come and go. You hold within your spirit all the thousand sorrows and the thousand joys of living. You look down upon the lovers, the boys, and smile. They, and the moon, and the river, and you…will be here. Forever.

CHAPTER 1

The marble mantel clock stops its ticking at the moment of Oscar Wilde's last breath, and in the silence that follows one can hear the sound of unwritten books snapping shut forever.

A young man, dark and fine of feature, distinguished by a heroically arched nose, moves swiftly to the bedside. His name is Timothy Tyharde. He feels for a pulse, knowing what he will find. He moves Oscar's head slightly to the left so that the glazed eyes no longer survey the offending wallpaper, but instead look upwards in a puzzled stare. He closes the eyes.

"It is finished," Timothy confirms to the small assembly. He concentrates his attention on Robbie Ross. This dear, slight man, Timothy knows, is a true friend to Oscar in life, and past death; a man devoted, a man to be trusted for last things: to see Oscar's coffin buried in a proper grave, to attend to his literary estate with the utmost of care, and, in time, to settle his outstanding debts. Robbie begins his generosity with two French coins, which he hands over to Timothy, to be placed upon Oscar's lids.

Robbie Ross is the first to turn away in tears, followed closely by Reggie Turner who, in the preceding days and nights, has done yeoman's duty tending to poor Oscar who had been delirious from ear infection and brain fever. For Robbie and Reggie the terrible story is over.

Remaining with the corpse are Timothy and Lady Eleanora Ashburton, both recently arrived from London, and M. Dupoirier, the proprietor of the hotel wherein these sad events are unfolding, and who is weeping silently in a corner of the room he has given to Oscar, without recompense, for many months. With M. Dupoirier's sanction, Lady Eleanora Ashburton is quite competently disguised in the garb of a hotel chambermaid. Timothy appears as himself. The three conspirators are now free to proceed with their furtive work.

Lady Eleanora speaks: "M. Dupoirier, dry your tears. We must begin at once."

—⤳—

A short distance away, in another part of Paris, the renowned sculptor, Auguste Rodin, stands alone in his large, light-filled studio and surveys his latest work with satisfaction.

Except for the undue haste required by the circumstances—he had been given but a few days notice—the commission had, at first, appeared to be a simple one: to sculpt the form of a dead man, conforming to a particular height as was often the case in monuments. The commission also specified, and this was the odd part, a particular weight. Weight ruled out the use of stone or marble, the usual materials for an effigy.

Rodin had listened with concentration to the requests of the man, Timothy Tyharde, an intense young Scotsman with a scything nose who commissioned the sculpture, and Rodin had watched with interest the handsome unnamed Englishwoman who accompanied him but who, Rodin could discern, was not in love with her escort. She had been, in fact, a little smitten with himself, he thought, and appeared somewhat in awe. Rodin had smiled at this. He liked to inspire awe in a lady.

Rodin had seen no evil in the couple's unusual request, and the chance for a great deal of good. A substantial amount of money had been offered as well—his intuition told him that it came from the woman—and it would be helpful to him, particularly as it was to be paid in real English sterling, not in false French promises. However, it was the work itself that interested him, and the help it might be to a friend. So it was with pleasure that he had shaken the hand of the nervous young gentleman. With even more pleasure he had kissed the hand of the lady. Rodin had begun to work before their carriage left his courtyard.

The question of weight had been a puzzle, for he had heard that the weight of a dead man was far heavier than what it had been in life. Why this should be so he could not make out, and he could not bring himself to believe it. Still, it was a puzzling idea and so he had consulted with an undertaker on the matter, an unpleasant little gnome of a man who knew he was speaking to a famous artist and a great intellect and, therefore, a perfect fool. The undertaker had explained very slowly and very politely and very offensively that although no gain in weight actually accrued at death, the reluctance of a body to participate in its own lifting, to mold itself in any way that might assist the efforts of the living, accounted for the illusion of increased weight. This amused Rodin. A dead man, when you carried him, was exactly like his monument.

Then with his hands upon the clay, he worked from memory, modeling a man far from beautiful, but prepossessing nonetheless. As he worked his mind turned as it often did at such times, to dark thoughts. He had recently heard of the mortal illness of his but newly found friend, the writer and wit, Oscar Wilde.

Auguste Rodin, like Wilde, was a man of great fame and fortune, whose amorous improprieties were, unlike those of the unfortunate English writer, taken for granted and excused by the French society in which he had prospered. Rodin's sins were with women, many women, but he had certainly looked at men's bodies closer than anyone alive.

What if, Rodin had pondered, what if, for my lack of sexual discretion I were to lose everything, as did Oscar Wilde? Oh, not just my renown, but my wife as well, and my home, and all my precious books and works of art, and the right to even see my own offspring? What if my very name was stripped from my family, torn like a signature from the canvas of their lives? Oscar Wilde, by all accounts, had fathered two sons whom he loved very dearly and longed for very much, whereas Auguste Rodin had only one whom he disliked heartily, but no matter. These incongruities did not impede his imaginative descent.

What if I, like Oscar Wilde, dismantled the remaining honor of an already dubious but once respectable family name? What if, in my hour of need, almost all of my friends abandoned me? And what if my freedom was denied me, and while I was in prison my beloved mother and my only brother both died, and my wife fell ill, and my manservant was hanging dead from a roof beam? All destroyed, by the shame I brought upon their heads.

Rodin knew that other people indulged in this kind of gruesome fantasy when they heard tell of the tragedies of others. Much of the popular press throve upon the incitement of vicarious suffering. He knew that such speculation offered a perverse pleasure; it was, after all, relieving to know you were *not* the person thrashing about in the throes of suffering. One could take an odd relief that one's own trials were not so severe, not so horribly present. Or, perhaps, it was a kind of rehearsal for the future catastrophes that every man knows await him along the path of life's journey. Pleasure was not Rodin's aim in taking his imaginary perambulation in the terrible ill-fitting shoes of Oscar Wilde. His contemplation served a greater purpose. His hands, as they plied the clay, began to ache. He went on working. He went on thinking.

And what if all my works of art were removed from public view, and my income, what remained to me, was taken to pay the legal expenses of the very man who had hounded me into the law courts and into the prisons? What if, in the resulting bankruptcy, my home was invaded, and all my beautiful possessions were sold at auction and carried off by an ignorant mob? Sweat broke out upon his brow.

What if during those years in prison, serving a sentence for a crime that was not a crime but a private erotic proclivity, what if I was put to hard labor to which I was physically unsuited so that my health as well as my heart was broken? This was the hardest of the afflictions for Rodin to envision for he was a stronger man than Oscar Wilde, not at all effete. Rodin had been made resilient by the years in which he had wrestled with clay and hammered at stone; and so to find and feel empathy with Oscar, who had been put to hard labor he pictured himself, Auguste, forced to embroider fine tapestries with a thin needle in poor light until his eyes grew dim.

And what if the materials that I needed for my artistic work were denied me, and even the privacy of my correspondence was read and censored?

His muscular arms throbbed with his work.

What if my lover, on whose behalf I had been pilloried, had not once written to me while I labored in prison; not one letter to ease the endless days and nights of solitary confinement, and had instead sold my private correspondence to the newspapers, and my personal gifts to the pawnbrokers to support his gambling habit?

The tortured clay within his grasp began, at last, to respond.

What if upon the day of my release from jail, broken in spirit and in bodily health, I was hounded by so hostile a press and so vicious a public that I was forced to flee my own country, assume a false identity, and then, without having been reunited with my wife, I heard that she, too, had died?

And then, the worst of all, to discover in the remains of my own shattered heart a most terrifying emotion, love that kept me bound to my lover, the very cause of my disgrace, and with whom I was destined to continue what brief life I had left before me, enchained by the remains of remorseless passion.

As Rodin pursued these dark imaginings, the figure beneath his fingers convulsed in an agony conveyed through his own muscle and sinew.

When he stepped back to observe the whole of his work he saw not the form of a vibrant living man but the effigy of the haggard and haunted man he had last glimpsed only weeks before. A thing better off buried. Dust to dust, said the English, ashes to ashes. Clay to clay.

Yet the figure had not entirely pleased him. Something deep in the back of his mind was trying to free itself, like a form from a stone.

After a solitary supper of cold meat and Burgundy, Auguste Rodin had made his way along the corridor to his bedroom. His current mistress awaited him in the next chamber, but he did not make his usual journey to her side. He slept alone, restless for the morning. He awakened with an image from his dreams, an image of a spade biting into the earth, a heavy foot pushing the blade deeper and deeper, and the sound of the shovel hitting long-buried wood. He knew then what was troubling him about the figure. And he knew what he must do.

He worked then with a kind of fever, for he had never before tried to achieve such a figure. At last, arriving at a likeness that suited him, he set to work covering the clay model in a blanket of wet plaster which, when dry, broke neatly into two parts like a well-tapped eggshell, and out of which he scooped the clay before sealing the plaster mold together again. Through a small hole in the top he now poured a silt mixture of his own devising—part clay, part sand, part cloth fiber with a wheat flour adhesive—which, if his calculations proved correct, would dry to an almost perfect human weight.

By the end of the week he had liberated the figure from its tomb of plaster, and after several more days of work with chisel and file the horrifying effigy was complete. He knew the sorrowful sculpture would never be known, never be seen by his public. But yet…but yet…he was an artist. So taking up a small chisel, he had signed it. *Auguste Rodin.*

The carriage pulling the wagon with the heavily draped coffin made its way across Paris towards Rodin's atelier. Inside the carriage, Timothy and Eleanora stared at each other, willing the next hours to pass swiftly and without incident. Inside the coffin, the still form of Oscar Wilde bumped about, none too gently.

"Has M. Dupoirier done his work?" asked Lady Eleanora.

"All that can be done," replied Timothy.

"The coroner has been paid?"

"Well."

The old horses put to the slow task of funerals proceeded into Rodin's courtyard. They were pulled up next to the atelier, and stopped.

By the time Timothy had helped Eleanora to the ground, Rodin was beside them peering at the coffin with intense interest. "I will help you," was all he said, and together with the driver they removed the heavy box, took it into the studio and deposited it with an echoing thud upon the stone floor.

Timothy gave the driver instructions to return after a short interval, handed him money for wine, and watched as he left the courtyard, a happy if somewhat bewildered figure in faded black.

Auguste Rodin, Lady Eleanora and Timothy now stood alone around the coffin.

"First let us see what you have wrought M. Rodin," requested Eleanora.

"With pleasure, Madame," August replied. "It is there, behind you."

She turned and Rodin quickly pulled back a covering sheet. Both Eleanora and Timothy gasped. The sight of Rodin's completed sculpture lying upon the table was a shock. He himself had blanched at the grim visage of death and deterioration.

"Why this is more than we anticipated, M. Rodin. We imagined only having a crude likeness given the lack of time, not a work of art. What perfection! What attention to detail! What decay! How did you accomplish it?"

Rodin was pleased, and bowed slightly to Eleanora. "It does not repel you?" he queried.

"No more than does *The Picture of Dorian Gray* repel me. They are both beautiful works of art on dreadful subjects. You have done Mr. Wilde a great honor."

"I am sorry we must be in such haste," prodded Timothy, "but Oscar's friends are waiting for us at the church. We must not delay or we will arouse suspicion."

Without further comment they turned to the task of prying up the nails of the coffin, Lady Eleanora working alongside the two men.

The lid was lifted off.

The three conspirators peered inside, holding their collective breath. Rodin's bearded face leaned close to Oscar's and removed the cloth that held the two coins in place. He then removed the coins. The eyelids of the corpse began to flutter in the sudden light. One eye blinked open, then the other.

"Auguste Rodin!" said Oscar, "whatever are you doing here?"

"This is my studio."

"Well then, what am I doing here?"

"You're not. You're dead."

"'But in that sleep of death, what dreams may come...?' Still, I shouldn't have thought I would dream of you."

"Why don't you let me help you out of that box?"

"Oh, I never arise before noon."

Auguste Rodin laughed heartily. "Perhaps you would like to make an exception in this case?"

"I make an exception of myself in every case, but it befits ill men to be recumbent, so perhaps you will tell me what the devil is going on and, while you are at it, open another bottle of that excellent Bordeaux you shared with me when last I dined at your table. I remember how its scarlet radiance caught the candlelight. It was like drinking liquid rubies."

"Come, let us help you," said Eleanora tenderly. But by the time the words were spoken, Oscar was unconscious again.

"This is a job for me," declared Rodin.

With his great sculptor's arms he reached into the casket, removing Oscar as easily as a baby from a cradle. He put Oscar's inert form upon the floor in a sun-warmed corner of the studio. Timothy and Eleanor worked swiftly to remove Oscar's clothes, handing them to Rodin who carefully fitted them onto the sculpture. Just as carefully Eleanora, revealing no embarrassment, worked Oscar's sleeping body into a loose brown cassock.

Rodin lifted his sculpture from the worktable and placed it into the coffin. There was one last moment when they all peered at the figure, and then with a deft hand, Rodin lifted the coffin's lid into place. Timothy was ready with the hammers, and together they drove the nails back into place.

Oscar, meanwhile, was having a beautiful dream. In his dream he lay within a cushion-lined casket of polished mahogany with silver handles and clasps. He wore a suit of emerald green velvet and a creamy satin shirt with a silk tie of the most delicate mauve. On his fingers were many rings made of gold and precious rubies, the color of Bordeaux, which glittered in the light of a thousand candles. The casket was placed on the high altar of St. Peter's in Rome. Bosie, his lover, was weeping like an angel beside him, and the cathedral was filled with his friends who had multiplied themselves, like the loaves and the fishes, until the enormous space was overflowing with mourners.

Meanwhile the coachman's returning footsteps rang upon the cobblestones. The men hoisted the coffin.

Eleanora hovered over Oscar in his sunny slumber. "Oscar is smiling in his sleep," said Eleanora. "I have not seen him smile so peacefully for a very long time."

So that is whom she loves, thought Rodin. Poor thing. He thought it a waste of a lovely woman when there were lusty men, such as him, alive and willing to be of service. Men's love of men had always seemed thoroughly beside the point to Rodin. There was great pleasure to be made between men and women, and one got babies too, as reward or punishment, in a most amusing form of bourgeois justice.

"This is awfully heavy," gasped Timothy to Rodin, sagging at his end of the coffin. Rodin chuckled, and took on a little more of the weight himself. With the help of the wagon driver they heaved the box up and into place, and in the next instant Timothy had climbed into the carriage.

"Thank you, thank you," he cried to Rodin. "Oscar has a true friend in Auguste Rodin."

"And in you. I hope to see you again soon, Mr. Tyharde," called out Rodin as the carriage with the closed coffin enclosing the effigy pulled away, "under less hurried circumstances."

Another carriage immediately entered the courtyard, and together Rodin and Lady Ashburton helped the semi-comatose Oscar to climb inside. "Thank you, my dear M. Rodin," said Lady Ashburton, and good to her word and his intuition, she placed a small sack of silver into his hand.

"Come back soon," said Rodin, "and I shall make art of you."

"What a lovely thought," she replied, but Rodin could see that her true concern was with Oscar and the journey that lay ahead. Once Oscar was settled upon the red leather seat of the carriage next to dear Eleanora who, it seemed to Oscar, was having an *affaire de coeur* with Rodin, he leaned his aching head against the little pillow that she provided and knew no more for three days' time, and when he did he was frightfully hungry.

CHAPTER 2

The Memoirs of Aveline Tartine

My mother could have drowned me I suppose. Instead she left me, on the first day of my life, to Fate. Could she have imagined that Fate and I would travel together for over a century? I think she did not think of me at all, so I have had to do this thing, thinking of me, for two. I have just passed my hundred-and-first birthday, though perhaps you should not trust a woman entirely on the subject of her age, no? I look into my mirror as I put on the rose from a jar. It is not so nice, this face with the withered cheek. I wear a copper-colored dress of satin with a high, lace-encumbered collar. It flatters me. I am both fascinated and repelled by the evidence of my ruined beauty.

I have decided to tell my stories, not because I have any particular affection for you young people of today, you men of business, you liberated women, but because I feel a debt to history. I *am* history.

I met Oscar Wilde when he was the most unpopular man in the world, a year or two after his release from Reading Gaol; and he was officially dead when I succeeded to know him well. Now... *Voilà!* He is popular. He would have relished this little trick of Fate, this belated gift of Irony.

Let your eyes see what my eyes see: the room in which I sit, unchanged in appearance since the turn of the century, except for the discreet installation of electric lights though, like Oscar's mother, Lady Wilde, I prefer candles. Behind the walls covered in watery silks and leprous brocades lurks the modern plumbing. Of this I approve. Striped sofas and flowered draperies fight ferociously for prominence, worn Oriental carpets smother the parquet floors, tight-necked urns choke clumps of cabbage roses whose fallen petals lie dead upon the tabletops. It is in this house, after the mad departure of Rodin's mistress, Camille Claudel, and several others of ill repute, that I have presided for seventy-seven years. I have been happy here.

You should have seen it as I first saw it, La Folie Neufbourg. Oh, it appeared dilapidated from the outside, even then. So it was kept. Inside was kept its secrets. You have heard the phrase, "glittering salons," yes? The phrase is used to excess in the popular press: glittering salons, brilliant soirées…what do you know? La Folie Neufbourg was known as the house of candles. There was a small shed in the garden, where, every day, the candles where made. Every night they were lit…one hundred, two hundred, three hundred…and onward…by a dozen servants who arrived at the dusk only for this task. And those who came here to sit within their glow, they glittered, too.

All the best minds, all the best talents of Paris once filled these rooms. Such men! I was young then, and unformed. They were older, accomplished, and this made them very glamorous to my eye. It is best to prefer the older man, I think. He has painted his masterpiece already, but maybe you will inspire another. A romantic notion that quickens the blood, yes? Of course the women they came also. Charming women. Charming as snakes, some of them. Ah, but the men! Renoir. He traveled here on his steam tricycle one night all the way from Saint-Cloud. How we laughed at him and his little machine. "Full speed behind," said Oscar Wilde, when he saw him coming into the courtyard.

Wilde poked a good deal of fun at Claude Monet as well, who sat with an axe by his plate. Yes, an axe. Would the local authorities attempt to cut down his trees? Monet bellowed. They needed wood. If they tried, he declared, he would cut down the authorities themselves. It was an obsession. What a pity to waste obsession upon trees. But they were all obsessed…with trees, with the sky, with the water, and most of all, with the light. The art, it obsessed them.

Some of the men, they were obsessed with one another's women, as well. Not Oscar Wilde, of course. But I precede myself.

Auguste Rodin believed that everything in this house was alive. This vase...this brush...those small nudes painted by Cezanne...nothing was inanimate, nothing was empty.

Inside the object there lurked a spirit, sometimes many spirits. The challenge was how to find them. It is a puzzle, no? But to Auguste Rodin, the spirits came. The trees talked to him and the clouds gave up their secrets. When he painted he heard the cries of his paints, the whispers of his brushes and he told their tales to the canvas. When he sculpted, he sensed the life in the stones, and gave their stories form. It is better, I think, to be the subject of a work of art than the author of one. Then you will live forever. I believed that when I was very young, when I sat as a model for those nude studies. I have not changed my mind. I almost never change my mind.

So now you have the setting, the atmosphere, for my story. Yes? The one I will tell you of Oscar Wilde. He was dear to me and often came to visit Auguste and me, here in this now crumbling mansion, where I grew to womanhood—with no help from any woman, but with the attention of several great men. Auguste was very fond of Oscar and always welcomed him into our home with the warmest of hearts for Oscar felt that the damp Venetian winters were taxing upon his health, and I expect they were too reminiscent of the dank prison that had once broken him, body and soul, though here, with us, he seemed content in the secret chambers.

In Paris, everything is either fashionable or unfashionable, and therefore it is either done, or it is not done. It has always been so. You must inform yourself of all the fashions of the society in which you move, no? Oscar Wilde was, for a while—after his resurrection—the fashion, which suited his character perfectly. In the years of which I speak, the early years of the new century, he had, of his own accord, chosen to resurrect himself, not as his flamboyant former self, but secretly. Anyone who was anyone in the artistic and literary community of Paris kept his secret. Vuillard, the dull little man who painted only the mother the sister the friends, kept the secret. Gide did, though it almost killed him to be discreet for he was a gossip by nature, and pretended not to like Oscar, when in fact he was smitten of him. The dreadful Austrian, Rilke did, and Renoir, and that scoundrel, Degas, who actually had the nerve to disapprove of him; they all kept silent. We were a scandalous lot when it came to our precious secret, the petite bourgeois artists of the *fin de siècle* with their pet recluse. They are all gone now.

I, alone, remain…with my stories, my collection of letters, even a lost manuscript. This is intriguing, yes? Look out the window there. Do you see that ancient hazelnut tree? Yes? It is along the limbs of that tree when, as a young girl, I made my escape from the Convent of the Sacred Heart just on the other side of the wall. I had for years been climbing out upon the convent's roof to see the comings and goings of La Folie Neufbourg. These people, they appealed to me. It took me a long while to make out what they were up to but at last I conceived the notion that I would become Rodin's model. I did not know his name, of course.

It was the spring of nineteen hundred, the year of the great Paris Exposition, and Oscar Wilde was still officially alive though he traveled under the assumed name of Sebastian Melmoth. Few would entertain him, as he was deep in delicious disgrace. He was a great admirer of the sculpture of Rodin. He had called Auguste the greatest living French poet, who had outshone even Victor Hugo. Auguste liked the accolade and had him to dinner, disgrace be damned. Later Auguste told me that Oscar had turned from the parlor window and said, "Look Auguste, a small brown, and rather appealing animal has jumped into your garden from the hazelnut tree," and Rodin came out of the house and picked me up and brushed me off while Oscar watched from the window. Ah, the touch of Rodin…so rough and so gentle all at once. I had never known the touch of any man before.

"What are you doing here?" he asked me.

I was quivering, partly from the shock of the jump, but I hid it well. "I wanted to see. I fell from the branch that comes over your wall."

"Are you hurt?"

"No."

"It will not do," he declared.

"What will not do?" I challenged.

"It will not do to lie to me. You quite willfully jumped from that tree. Admit that this is so."

"Yes."

"Have you any money in that little basket?" he asked me.

"None at all."

"Just as I expected. If attractive young women are to fling themselves into my garden I wish they would do so carrying baskets of gold so they could be properly cared for."

He was the first person to ever compliment me and I was emboldened by his words. "I can work for my keep."

"I have too many servants already, both here and at my home in Meudon where my family lives. Two houses to maintain! Still my wife, Rose, must be made comfortable in her home and…the others here, in this one. And, they must be kept comfortably apart. Women who are comfortable cause a man less trouble, but much expense."

"I could be your model."

"What do you know of this? You are only a child." He looked me over in a way that made me blush. "Besides you are too thin. What did they feed you in that convent? No, don't tell me. I don't want to know."

"If you don't want me here, I'll go. I can make my own way in the world."

"Now you threaten me with your own ruin. What trouble will fall next from the trees? I suppose you can stay until we figure out what to do with you. Perhaps your presence will raise the tone of the establishment. A religious presence is rare here."

"I am not religious. I don't believe in any of it. I have a mind, you know." I clutched the small, wooden crucifix that hung on a string around my neck and pulled hard at it, breaking the string. I flung the hateful cross into the rose bushes.

"A mind is of equivocal value in a woman. Come along, I'll give you over to someone who can see to you. And please do not litter my garden further with your totemic artifacts. Unless they are of great beauty, of course."

He slipped his great hand around my bony wrist, and I followed him into the house without protest. In the kitchen the cook gave me a cup of strong black tea. Two housemaids strutted around me, clucking like peahens. Rodin said simply, "Feed this girl and look after her," and turned to leave the kitchen. At the door, he turned back. "What are you called?"

"I don't know my true name," I replied. "At the convent, where I was taken in as an infant, I was given the name of Angelique."

He shook his head. "Angelique will not do. You are too willful to be an Angelique, though you fall from the skies. You have escaped the good Sisters of the Sacred Heart, and doubtless in so doing you have also escaped the heavenly realms for which your name intends you."

There was the quiet stir of servants as they crossed themselves.

"You have abandoned yourself to the earthier ways of this poor world," continued Rodin. "I will give you another name. I shall call you Aveline."

"Aveline? What does it mean? I've never heard it before." I stared at him, perplexed.

"It is old French. It means hazelnut."

Then I smiled at him, pleased with the idea. Rodin did not return the smile. He left the kitchen abruptly, as if to escape our small intimacy. My heart was pounding. I had fallen twice in ten minutes—out of the hazelnut tree, and into love with Auguste Rodin.

All the servants made quite a fuss over me, especially Madeleine who was to become my lady's maid in due time. They decided to put me in a back bedroom near the kitchens and to bring me some discarded dresses of the current mistress of the house, a woman named Sophie, I believe, or maybe it was Isabelle. No matter. I made short work of her, whoever she was. I was drinking my tea thinking only of Rodin's voice and touch, when Oscar Wilde, who was a stranger to me in every way, came into the kitchen.

The servants fell silent and looked askance, so I sensed there was something louche about him. He was big, with large soft features, which I judged to be ugly, as I had just fallen in love with an older, harder, bearded colossus. I remember thinking I must have jumped into a land of giants.

"So this is the little squirrel who has scampered into our lives."

"I'm not a squirrel, I'm a girl," I declared with the sauciness that had gotten me into worlds of trouble in the convent.

"And a budding poetess, too." He laughed. It was a wonderful laugh. "It seems you have fled the Penguins of Sacred Heart for the Peacocks of Sacred Art. I am Mr. Oscar Wilde, currently unknown as M. Sebastian Melmoth. I, too, write poetry, of somewhat more substantial length. And whom do I have the pleasure of meeting?"

"I used to be Angelique, but M. Rodin says I am to be Aveline."

"So we have each adopted a false name. Auguste has replaced your Christian name with a pagan one. I consider it most suitable. But what is your family name?"

"I haven't one. I am a foundling. I was abandoned on the steps of the convent when I was only one day old."

He suddenly appeared concerned. "You weren't by any chance left in a handbag, were you?"

"A handbag? No. I was found in a basket," I replied, eager to allay his strange anxiety.

"Well, that is a great relief to me."

"I still have the basket. My few things are in it. Here." I held up the little basket that contained an infant's nightdress, a rosary, and the rag of a blanket. "Why?"

"Fate sometimes exhibits a peculiar friendship for Irony. I was afraid she was having me on."

I could make nothing of this reply for I was, of course, entirely ignorant of *The Importance of Being Earnest* with its foundlings and handbags. I had never even heard the name of Oscar Wilde, so sheltered had I been.

"So you had no mother?"

"The sisters did their best to mother me."

"A sister is not a proper mother."

Oscar abruptly turned his attention to the servants. "Madeleine, bring me a nice cup of chocolate." The maid curtsied, and moved away to her task. My eyes must have grown large at the thought. "Make that two cups of chocolate, please," he said. "Tea is not a felicitous drink in France. Sit down here, Aveline, we have momentous work to attend to."

He indicated a place for me at a side table and I sat down across from him, curious. I was sustained by the anticipation of the chocolate, which I had tasted only once before, but remembered with intense pleasure.

"Now I have some knowledge of foundlings, though rightly they should be referred to as lostlings. You see, when I am not writing poetry or being put into prisons, I write plays and other works of fiction. Foundlings have an uncanny way of showing up in fiction, and have thus provided me with an excellent education on the subject. Now, one thing I have learned is that it is important that you acquire some relations. I, for instance, would be glad to serve as your Dear Uncle Oscar. I am lost in my own way and so make a suitable choice. You must think about this proposal carefully, for to be an orphan and, therefore, in the position to choose your own family is a great advantage. Of course, I am in social disgrace at this time, so I may not be an asset to you in your march through civilized life, except as a secret advisor."

I loved secrets, and to sweeten the idea the chocolate arrived. Madeleine brought a plate with a selection of small cakes in accompaniment. Oscar and I reached for the most luscious looking cake at the same time. Laughing again, Oscar broke the desired confection into two pieces and took the larger for himself. I smiled and took the smaller piece and a second cake as well.

"We are very well matched," he observed.

"Yes, I believe we are, Uncle Oscar."

"That makes me very happy. I should be happier still if you were to call me Dear Uncle Oscar. Now the next order of business is the assumption of a proper last name. This is also a matter of great importance. Your name cannot be Wilde, which is unfortunate, for Wilde would suit you very well, but, as I have indicated, it is a name currently in much disrepair. Why, I seldom use it myself, except on important occasions. And Aveline Melmoth is clumsy, don't you think? So let us consider what your name should be…Fairfax? Windermere? Bracknell? Or would you prefer something French, being French as you are, as it were?"

"I think I should prefer a French name, Dear Uncle Oscar."

"Now let's see…Balzac, Flaubert, Hugo—"

While he pondered, I helped myself to another cake. Oscar watched me with approval, then arriving at an idea continued, "You know, I had an excellent treat last night in a private room at Maxim's, as a friend of mine was lucky at horses and shared his well-gotten gains with me. The dessert was both sweet and savory and went by a most delicious name. It was called a tartine. Should we call you Aveline Tartine? What do you say?"

"As you please, Dear Uncle Oscar."

"As I please? Did the nuns teach you obedience? It's an outrage! Attempting to sully the character of a perfectly good child. Well, perhaps what damage is done can yet be undone. Never be compliant, Aveline. People will think you are nice. No one cares for nice people except other nice people and that makes for very dull company indeed. No one ever speaks about nice people in public, which is all that matters, and once they are dead, no one ever speaks of them at all which is as it should be."

"But I like the name Aveline Tartine."

"Well, in that case, if you don't mind going about the world with a name that belongs more properly on the dinner menu than the dinner invitation, Aveline Tartine it will be. It's a nice tasty name for the desirable woman you will soon become."

Something blazed up inside me at his words. Until that moment—through the long lonely years of my cloistered childhood—I had known only my own desires, among them the adoration of the Godlike beings I glimpsed in the garden of La Folie Neufbourg. There was something entirely new and hotly exciting about the idea of someone desiring me. I flushed.

"I see I have embarrassed you, Mademoiselle Tartine. I am sorry to have been so long about it. Pray forgive me."

I remember that I giggled. That, too was an entirely new experience for me. "You are making fun of me, Dear Uncle Oscar."

"I was merely making fun. I used to make fun…often. And perhaps, as I am out of practice, I no longer do it quite so perfectly. I try never to make anyone the butt of my jokes. To hurt others in the pursuit of humor is a German tradition and quite detestable."

"I've never met a German."

"That must account entirely for the sweetness of your nature. I think,

Aveline, we are to be very great friends for you bring out the worst in me and I treasure that quality in a friendship. I think I shall have another strawberry cake. Why, how excellent! You have eaten them all!"

Our meeting was interrupted by a loud knock on the kitchen door. The nuns had sent two priests after me. Like dogs they came, sniffing about in their black cassocks, but Oscar sent them away. He said, "It is too late to save the girl now, she has fallen." Horrified by the conjuring of their own minds they turned away.

"Give a man of God the opportunity to think and he will think of sin," said Oscar, smiling. "Now, Sebastian Melmoth must go out into the world of godless men for yet awhile. I look forward to our next meeting, my little hazelnut."

But the next time I heard tell of my Dear Uncle Oscar, I was informed, by a somber Auguste Rodin, that he was dead.

CHAPTER 3

The Venetian Lagoon

March 1901

The jonquils were thrilling. They arose from their earthy beds in the sheltered side of the garden and, holding their golden blooms aloft, ran happily across the greensward to meet the morning sun. They rippled in happy waves as they surrounded the ivy bed and the ancient wellhead. They raced without care up the slopes of a low embankment that held at bay an expanse of beryl-green water. There, at the very brink of the quiet sea, and heedless of propriety, they danced wildly in the full light of day. A fine emerald peacock joined them. How perfect, thought Oscar.

He could see the flowers and the strutting bird from his place at the narrow opening in the thick stone wall of the cell. It was a monk's cell. Unlike prison, it had whitewashed walls, a terrazzo floor, and a brightly lit lamp of brass and sparkling Murano glass. It was a cell decorated for a visitor of distinction. The floor was brightened with a fine carpet from Persia, deeply entrenched with color. The bed was covered with a yellow and white silk spread that had once graced his own bedroom in Tite Street, London. Lady Eleanora Ashburton had salvaged this coverlet, along with a few other precious possessions, from the bankruptcy sale—which had been more like a looting by an unruly mob, of his once delightful home. The House Beautiful, it had been dubbed, the House Ravaged, it had become. Eleanora had brought the coverlet with her on the long journey to this place of exile. He could hardly bear to look upon it.

Over the bed was a crucifix, the only adornment on the walls. Whenever he looked at it he remembered the prisoners still in the gaols in which he had been incarcerated: Holloway, Pentonville, Reading. Didn't Christ break bread with outcasts? This religious cell, like all cells, was given to dampness but, unlike the miserable cages of England, this one had fire against the damp, fighting to keep it warm and dry by night and day.

Through the open doorway, the door itself being a work of carved and polished wood, he could hear the monks at evensong. Their rhythmical Latin was soothing to his spirit. A bottle of a mellow red vino da tavola, a slice of finely aged Romano cheese, and a small loaf of freshly baked bread were arranged on a silver tray that sat upon the rough-hewn table in the center of the room. Fine utensils were placed next to the tray and next to these a tin box held writing supplies, never touched. Beneath the window a bookcase embraced a dozen carefully chosen, unopened volumes bound in fine leather, among them the works of Shakespeare, Chaucer, and Milton, Dante in the original Italian, and a copy of the Gospels, in Greek, very like the volume that had sustained him through the first foul months in Reading Gaol. Two chairs, one plain, one carved in an excessive Venetian manner, completed the furnishings. A hook behind the door held a spare cassock and a cloak. He had everything he needed and nothing he wanted.

Following the curious experiences of his death and return to life, his strange jolting ride inside the pine coffin through the streets of Paris to Rodin's courtyard, and the sleep-blackened journey across the continent, Oscar had awakened in this isolated monastery and almost immediately fallen into a deep depression, unbroken throughout the long winter months of his physical recovery.

He had gained consciousness shortly after his arrival, miserable with hunger and thirst but too weak even to cry out. A mute and smiling friar in a coarse brown cassock, such as he now wore himself, sat patiently by his bedside and, on seeing that Oscar was awake, brought him a tray with cool water and a strong hot broth into which he had broken a slice of rich peasant bread. After Oscar had eaten, it was this monk who bathed his feverish brow, thus beginning the prolonged task of restoring him to his health.

At first Oscar had no idea where in the world he had been taken, and as the brothers kept the silence for all but an hour before retiring—an hour in which he did not see them—it was some time before he was certain that he was in Italy, though he had surmised that the air could be no other.

There was no one in this place that he knew. Timothy, Eleanora, the kind hotelier Dupoirier, and dear Auguste Rodin seemed but figments of a dream melted away with the dawn, and before them he recalled only nightmares. He was alone, set adrift in time and space, borne upon the soulful chants from without his chamber, barely responsive to the kindly ministrations of Fra Ricardo—for he finally did persuade the elderly friar to say his name.

Of course there was Prudence. Her faint but unrelenting voice instructed him not to exert himself or to protest in any way, to eat what was put before him, and drink his bitter medicinal teas without a fuss, and, in time, following her good counsel he was able to walk slowly around the cloister, wrapped in a woolen cape, with Fra Ricardo for support.

Oscar's naturally resilient body responded to the quiet and to the care, but his mood darkened and chilled with the weather and soon lay beneath a layer of thickening ice.

All that he loved was lost. And, worse, he could not imagine himself ever capable of loving anyone or anything again. Prudence had but one word to say upon the matter—wait.

In prison, with no caring soul to comfort him, he had not lost all heart; indeed his heart was full of feeling. In gaol he had loved and longed and grieved for all those who were kept apart from him. He had suffered the agonies of guilt and shame and remorse. And—except for one brief and hellish spell—he had refused the lure of directing his bitterness and hatred towards others, though he had often raged and seethed as he considered his own multitude of failures. Once, in utter darkness, he had thought to make a friend of suicide, but had turned away from death's minion in disgust. He, who had once said that suicide was the highest compliment one could pay to Society, found that he did not wish to pay compliments, least of all to Society.

Here in this cell of comfort, wrapped in quiet safety and gentle regard, he relinquished every emotion. And here, if such a thing can be said without contradiction, he felt nothing. He went through the habits of living—with Prudence insisting and Fra Ricardo assisting—but inside himself he was the dead man whom the entire world, save his four absent friends and these kindly brothers, believed was lying in French dirt. That much he had surmised.

Images of his past, of happier times, passed through his mind occasionally. He remembered mornings at play along the edges of England with Cyril and Vyvyan, his two darling sons, who were delighted by his extravagant sand castles. He recalled the nights of uncorked wit and bubbling champagne in the midst of London's highest society. And he visited his youthful afternoons upon the precious green slopes of Ireland and the quadrangles of Oxford. He could contact no feeling in regard to any of these memories. They seemed to be the memories of some other man.

Images of horror and humiliation arrived as well, usually during the black, sleepless periods of the night, but these too were but a passing show, the narrative of some other being, about whom he cared not a bit. He entertained no desires, except for simple bodily urges and even these were dull.

Fra Ricardo warmed and watered him like a carefully tended plant that nevertheless, week after week, droops in its corner and neither feels, nor offers, any joy. Oscar believed that he wanted to die.

Once, when a tepid sun was feeling its way through the cold grey mist of an early February afternoon, he had spoken to Fra Ricardo when the man appeared to remove Oscar's luncheon tray. "I am sorry to leave all of your kindness without payment," he whispered. "I can find no genuine feeling within me with which to thank you."

"I accept despair," came the unexpected reply. Fra Ricardo spoke in a slow and careful English, clearly learned in solitude, with a book. His voice was as deep as his large green eyes that looked directly into Oscar's.

"Despair?" At the word, Oscar had begun to tremble.

"You have died almost from the struggle to feel not the despair. Let it have you. Do not be ashamed. It is a thing that must be done."

The look of permission in the man's eyes shredded the shroud of unfeeling within which Oscar had smothered his pain. He slowly fell to his knees, then curled in agony into a fetal position near the foot of the bed. A cry of horror escaped his lips, repeating itself over and over in his echoing brain. "Why? Why? Why? Why?"

His cry became the cry of all his torment, and not of his torment alone. It became the Why of all Whys. Why do children die? Why do animals suffer? Why do men torture one another? Why does death stalk the edge of the campfire's glow waiting to carry off the ones we love into the darkness?

No answer came. But he felt the presence of the calm Fra Ricardo above him, accepting his unmanly cries, staying with him while his tears broke from their prison of flesh and flowed upon the unyielding floor. An hour passed, and passed again, before his weeping subsided.

Exhausted, Oscar was helped to his bed and covered gently with the beautiful coverlet, and, for the first time, found comfort in it. Fra Ricardo then crossed himself silently and left Oscar alone. Oscar's soul had begun to recover.

And on this day, when the first tentative breeze of spring rippled the newly opened jonquils, Oscar smiled. The smile was observed by Fra Ricardo who, after gathering up his herbs and powders, took the smile to the Abate Antonio. The Abate brought it back to Oscar.

"So I hear that you have finally decided to join us, Mr. Wilde," said the Abate as he entered the chamber without the humble knock that always preceded Fra Ricardo. "You could not have chosen a day more apt. I am Abate Antonio, the Dupoirier of this remote hotel."

The sound of a perfectly spoken sentence in fluent Cambridge English shocked the already startled Oscar. He had never seen this man before but deduced his position as Abate from the combination of his dress and demeanor. The Abate wore the same simple cassock of the other monks, but his was of a new and finer cloth. The *tau* that fell from the chain at his neck was of ivory, and from his rope belt hung a large silver hoop that clutched a dozen iron keys.

The Abate was a man of about sixty; a big man, as tall as Oscar. His face was tanned to the golden brown of a seaside sophisticate. It bore no sign of the dank winter through which they had just passed. The look in his eyes was one of intelligent amusement, and the creases of age about the eyes were those of a man given to a cheerful disposition. It was a face that spoke of a contentment with life as he found it. The man unsettled Oscar, but years of social grace were not entirely forgotten. He shook the man's hand with the weak but warm grasp of the past.

"Why do you say that today is apt?" he asked.

"Today the swallows will return." The Abate reopened the door and pointed to the rafters of the cloister outside Oscar's room. For the first time Oscar noticed the small shelves, crudely made and attached to the ancient timbers just an inch or two below the roof. "This we call the Cloister of the Swallows. Soon the birds will be here to make new nests and carry on their lives amongst us. We Franciscans find a small miracle in their annual return. And now we find a small miracle in the return of your smile. It is our way."

"I have lost my way," replied Oscar. "Perhaps I shall adopt yours."

"That is not at all a bad thing for you to consider," observed the Abate. "Our life here is peaceful. But it has its excitements, too. Our novices, for instance, are allowed to leave the island once a year. They go to the neighboring island of St. Erasmus to see how the artichokes are coming up."

Oscar smiled again. It might, he thought, be possible to develop a fondness for this man. "But why am I here, of all places" he queried, "among religious men, of all people?"

"The Lord has put you here."

"That is not an answer I can understand."

"Then there is no answer," said the Abate.

"May I leave this place?"

"Of course. Where would you go?"

It seemed a genuine question. Oscar sighed. "Anywhere. It doesn't matter. I have no home now."

"That is not true. This is your home now." A look of concern passed across the Franciscan's face like the shadow of a bird. "If you leave us, how will you live?" he inquired.

"Does it matter to you?" challenged Oscar.

"It matters to God. And God and I have grown simpatico with one another's concerns."

"I shall hesitate to quarrel with you then. Where in all Italy am I?"

"You are upon the Isola San Francesco del Deserto in the Venetian lagoon."

Oscar gasped and turned ashen. The Abate placed a hand upon Oscar's shoulder and, responding to this slightest of pressures, Oscar sank into the nearby chair. The Abate settled himself into the chair opposite.

"I believe I can guess why you appear so changed by this news," he ventured.

"No one alive could know," declared Oscar.

"Oscar. May I call you Oscar? Surely you of all men cannot believe there are any secrets on this good earth."

"I pale at the knowledge of finding myself in so remote a prison. I once said I would end in the café or the cloister and I have arrived at the cloister. This cloister that will be my tomb if you hold me here."

"This is not a prison and you are not a prisoner. I will not have this place of refuge confused with a place of iniquity."

"Please accept my apology, Abate. I am quite undone."

"Your apology is accepted. And I believe you have come undone, as you say, upon hearing the name of this island because you still mourn for your little sister."

Oscar, amazed, stared at the Abate. "How could you know?"

"When you…how shall we say it? When you died in Paris, a paper was found on your person. On this paper you had written a poem; a poem to the memory of your dead sister. Now this poem has been published in England. There was no need to carry it about on a scrap of paper. You carried it with a lock of her hair, next to your heart—"

"Always." Oscar's hand went to the place where, even now, beneath his cassock, the locket rested against his chest.

"—and to nourish your heart. Her death was your heart's deepest wound. Your sister who died when she was only eleven and you were thirteen. And her name was—"

"—Isola Francesca."

"A small miracle, no? Perhaps your mother, poet that she was, had seen this name, Isola San Francesco, on a map and took license with it for the name of your little sister…or perhaps it is just a coincidence? To be brought, of all places, here? Let me tell you a line from another poem, one from the Song of Solomon. It goes like this: 'A garden locked is my sister, my bride, a garden locked, a fountain sealed.' Beautiful, isn't it? I think this might well describe your feelings for—"

"Isola Francesca," whispered Oscar.

"You do not wish me to say her name?"

"Her name is sacred to me."

"Its masculine counterpart is sacred here as well. Do you know how this island came to have its name?"

"This must be the island where St. Francis—? How does the story go?"

"St. Francis was traveling by sea along the coast of Italy, returning from his attempt in 1219 to evangelize the Muslims. Here, in the Venetian lagoon, his ship was assailed by a terrible storm and began to break apart. St. Francis was washed overboard. He was plucked from the thrashing waves by the gentle hand of God and let down upon this shore where he rested and recovered from his ordeal. Very like yourself."

"A legend?"

"One of several versions. The most ordinary is that he sailed here quite peacefully and found the island well suited for contemplation and prayer. We have in our archives a document ceding the island to St. Francis so we have roots in paper as well as in imagination."

"They go well together, paper and imagination."

The Abate rose and pointed at something through the small window. "Look there."

Oscar struggled to his feet and took his turn at the window.

"The stump there, in the center of the garden, is the base of a mighty tree that grew here for four centuries. It began its life as the staff of St. Francis, blossoming into life when he stuck it into the soil, claiming this place for God. Although the tree finally came down in a storm mightier than itself, we brothers can still see its branches protecting us. Now they shelter you. It is invisible, as faith is in invisible, as love is invisible."

Oscar sighed. To him the stump looked much the same as any other hunk of dead wood, and more nearly represented his ruined faith than the Abate's imaginative branches. He returned to the table in the center of the room and lifted the bottle of wine. He noticed that a second glass had been left on the tray. He poured for two and handed the Abate a glass. Then he sat down again. The Abate sat opposite. How strange, thought Oscar. They might, except for their robes, be members of a fashionable London gentlemen's club enjoying an afternoon's conversation.

"In prison I read the life of St. Francis," said Oscar.

"I have been told this thing." A moment of silence followed the Abate's words. The two men tasted their wine. It was the Abate's turn to sigh. "This is not the sort of table talk you are used to, I'm afraid."

"I am used to nothing."

"Forgive me. I should say, table talk that you were *once* used to, before the prison."

"Everything is gone from me. The three years since my release from Reading Gaol have been sordid. I have wandered about the continent, estranged from my family and from all those whom I loved. I have stayed in hotels that would have me only under an assumed name. Sebastian Melmoth. Is that not laughable? I have sat in cafés, unable to write anything charming, unable to love anything new, repeating old phrases to witless fools around me for lack of wit. And now, as you say, I am as shipwrecked as St. Francis. But I am not a saint. I am a sinner and one of the worst order of sinners because I do not repent my sins."

"And yet your sins have brought you to ruin."

A look of anger flashed in Oscar's eyes. "Other men's sins have brought me to ruin. Men's envy and hatred, their hypocrisy and need for a scapegoat, though they would call it...morality—their sins have brought me to ruin."

"And your own sins? Those you just spoke of—what have they done?"

"Why, they brought others to ruin. That is what sins do. They hounded and shamed my mother and my brother and my wife into the ground. Even my poor butler hung himself when I was convicted, for no honest work could be expected to come to the servant of Oscar Wilde. And my sins have forever corrupted the life of my dearest friend, Bosie Douglas, and will sully, but pray God, not destroy the lives of my own dear sons, those two precious innocents."

"And yet you do not see cause for repentance?"

"For the sake of those I have ruined? But I did not *know* they would be harmed. I was, right in the midst of what you and the world would call my sins, an innocent too. I thought my actions to be personal, and private and, as they were consensual, harmless but for the dark fascination they held for me, keeping me from my work, my sunlit pleasures. Had I known of their destructive power…had I known and continued in my…pursuits, why then I would be an evil man and no repentance could be enough in any case."

"But you were raised a Christian. You have studied Catholicism. You have always, even in what you call your innocence, known sin to be sin."

"I *knew* sin to be sin, but did not *feel* sin to be sin. I could not align my experience with what I had been taught by rote, and so I could not believe what I had been taught was true. I was, ironically, on a search for the truth. It was when I walked as a righteous man, a proper, married, English gentleman that I felt myself to be an impostor, a liar, and living in the tawdry disguise of truth. Can there be a greater sin than that?" He looked up, directly into the Abate's eyes. "May I speak frankly, Abate? I always thought confession should be eye to eye, by the way, not mouth to ear."

"I will listen to you, eye to eye," responded the Abate.

Satisfied, Oscar continued. "Then know that it was only when I held the form of a beautiful young man against my own skin that there existed no falsehood between myself and what God had made me to be. He made me thus. He made me so. He rewarded my honesty with the most exquisite pleasures I have ever known—hours of perfect joy, hours of purest ecstasy. How can I repent those moments when, in their very midst, I most felt that I was a creature of God's glory?"

Abate Antonio, good to his word, held eye contact with Oscar and answered him in a tone without condemnation, as though he were instructing a beloved child in the ways of the world. "This ecstasy was a deception of Satan, to disguise sin as God's intention for you. But you must have discovered, in these last five years of incarceration and exile that this was the Devil's ruse. You repented whilst you were on your deathbed. Was it a false confession?"

"When the priest came to me I was barely conscious, yet I could hear the rites and I was trying to speak, to say yes, yes, I love God and the gifts of this life, but no, no, I do not repent. I wanted to say, let the Almighty take me to his chambers as I really am, for though He may sit on a high bench and wear the wig of a judge and think, like an English judge that he is God, He *is* God. I was unable to form the words. It was most distressing. My friend Robbie Ross had always pushed me to become a Catholic. Robbie had always been a strong influence on me. He took my efforts at mumbled denials for affirmation, for that was his true heart's wish. He had confused my denials with wishes once before, a long time ago, and became my first male lover in the confusion. On my death bed, his intentions were loftier."

"Ah. I see. So you did not really wish to die in the faith?"

"Well, I did, actually."

"But then—"

"What I wish for, and what I can do are two very different matters." Oscar followed this pronouncement with a shrug of his shoulders. His expression was bemused.

"So what have I here? An unrepentant deathbed semi-convert?" asked the Abate.

"You have Oscar Wilde. And Oscar Wilde would have God, but also his sins. He would have his..." Prudence told him shut up.

"He would have his young men."

"Yes."

"And specifically Lord Alfred Douglas? Bosie, you call him?"

"Bosie is but a friend to me now. What we once were together is a glory faded."

The Franciscan sighed and sat for a long moment watching Oscar, who had closed his eyes to the present surroundings and seemed far, far away.

Then, silently making the sign of the cross, Abate Antonio arose to leave the man of infinite contradictions with his sorrows. At the door he turned once more. "Oscar, in this place myself and all the brothers sleep in our coffins at night. It is a preparation."

Oscar, roused from his reverie, took this in. "With all due respect, Abate Antonio, I have had enough of my coffin for one lifetime."

CHAPTER 4

A Note from Oscar Wilde
Regarding the Preceding Chapter

VENICE, ITALY
February 1912

Forgive me. I must pause and converse with you, my unknown reader, for you will remember that I was a man once renowned for his conversation. I require just a word before my departure for the new world.

I write to you in this memoir of my life and of my loves.

But, alas, the words are not made flesh. Printed words are not soft, pale skin and tender sighs. They are but ink and paper. You may kiss the page, but it will not compare with the gentle brush of rose red lips. You can never really know the pleasures I have known…unless, of course, you do.

CHAPTER 5

While the jonquils ran riot on Oscar's remote island, his friend and protector, Lady Eleanora Ashburton, muffled in a thick fur coat, stepped from the carriage at Berggasse 19 in Vienna. Looking neither right nor left, she took a steadying breath and rang the bell of the house directly in front of her. The door of the large, ordinary row house was opened by a discerning attendant who, having taken Eleanora's measure in one swift glance, motioned her inside and toward the staircase.

"The second floor, Madam."

"Thank you."

Eleanora gathered her skirts and ascended the stairs, noticing the smell of cooking meat as she passed the closed door on the first floor landing. Beef, she noted, and not a good quality beef, perhaps for a stew. This floor was where he lived. She hesitated a moment, trying to catch a sound from within the apartment. Hearing none, she continued upwards. Upon reaching the second floor, she paused to collect herself and to read the sign attached to the door:

Prof. Dr. Sigmund Freud

There was no bell, so she opened the door and entered into a comfortable waiting area filled with plush red furniture. White lace curtains veiled the windows, which overlooked a back courtyard. She declined to sit. Her heart was racing far faster than two flights of stairs could possibly warrant, but she wished to be standing when he appeared. She did not know why an erect posture seemed so important, but it did. She realized for the first time since making her decision to consult with this man that she was frightened. She knew perfectly well why she was here, but, what would she say? What would he hear?

Before she had time to contemplate the anticipated meeting further the door to the inner office opened. "Come in, Lady Ashburton, you are exactly on time," said Dr. Freud in a pleasantly accented English.

"Good day, Dr. Freud. Do you assign meaning to my promptness?" She noticed a slight quaver of nervousness in her voice and wondered if the doctor had detected it. "I have heard that for you everything has a hidden meaning, but I assure you, in this case, there is none. I was schooled to be punctual."

"There is a joke among my psychoanalytic colleagues, Lady Ashburton, that if a person arrives early she is anxious, late she is resistant, and on time, compulsive. Does that put you more or less on your guard? Eh?"

She smiled, feeling herself disarmed. "Less, to be sure, Dr. Freud."

He was shorter than she had imagined and he spoke with a beautiful voice she could not have anticipated. It was a compelling voice, almost as persuasive as Oscar's. She extended her gloved hand and felt it taken, gently, in his warm hand. He guided her over the threshold and into the inner office. She glanced quickly around the room. It was not to her taste, cluttered with books and *objets d'art* and archaeological artifacts, though everything was clean and free of dust. He kept a competent maid, she thought.

"Please be so kind as to sit here, in this chair. I know you have heard tales of my couch, but perhaps we should look each other in the eyes for a few minutes before we begin the treatment."

She sat down into an extremely comfortable chair. "Thank you, Dr. Freud, but I am not here for your treatments."

There was a slight raise of his left eyebrow. "Then how may I help you, Lady Ashburton?"

As she looked across into his compelling eyes, she felt her mind go quite blank. "I find that I don't know how to begin."

"If you did know how to begin, how do you imagine you would do so?"

She puzzled on this for a moment, then spoke. "I have come about a friend who needs your help."

"Ah yes, the friend. I know a few things about friends of this kind." Freud sat back in his chair. "Tell me about this friend."

"His name is Oscar Wilde. He was quite famous, now infamous. Perhaps you have heard of him?"

"Oscar Wilde, the English writer. Did I not read that he had died of the complications of an ear infection a short time ago? I recall the notice in the newspaper distinctly because the manner of his life and, particularly, the manner of his death, interested me. His father had been a famous physician, an ear surgeon, I believe."

"Why yes, Sir William Wilde was very well known, and a highly respected specialist. He developed the surgery for cataract removal, for he specialized in the eye as well as the ear."

"I recall thinking that Oscar Wilde must have suffered from a fatal lack of his father's attention."

"Oscar's father is long dead, Dr. Freud, but Oscar…what I say is in confidence?"

"My work depends upon it."

"Oscar Wilde is not dead."

Freud's left eyebrow rose again, ever so slightly.

"I am not mad, Dr. Freud. Oscar Wilde is believed to be dead. But he is alive and recovering on the Isola Francesco del Deserto in the Venetian lagoon. I took him there myself and I have made a donation to the monastery there for his keep."

Eleanora waited for a reaction. There was none. She felt a slight annoyance, mixed with disappointment, for this was the only person to whom she had told her tremendous secret and it had, apparently, been told to a man who didn't believe her.

She fished through her reticule and produced a letter. It was a brief note from Oscar, only two lines, confirming that he was physically improved, but capable of little more than breathing due to his melancholy. He had sent it in February, and it was the only word she had had from him during the months of his recovery. She handed the letter to Freud, who quickly perused it.

"This is signed 'with infinite affection, Sebastian Melmoth.'"

"Oh, that is Dear Oscar's assumed name. After his disgrace in England, no establishment, even on the continent, would house him under his own name. He took it from a novel entitled *Melmoth the Wanderer*, written, I believe, by a relation of his."

"Yes, I know the novel. It is not very good. Gothic. Doubtless 'Sebastian' is a reference to the greatly wounded saint."

"Yes."

"And St. Sebastian survived his injuries, did he not, at least for a time? Your story is of much interest to me, Lady Ashburton. Go on."

"I took him there—to Venice—because I loved him and because I believed the monks on the Isola Francesco Monastery might be able to cure him of his ear infection and the resulting brain fever."

"Yes. Venice is a romantic choice, so quite suitable. And these religious men, they have worked a cure?"

"Yes. As you see by the letter." Dr. Freud glanced again at the note. "If you overlook the melancholy," she added.

He put the note into its envelope, and handed it back to Eleanora.

"You say you loved him?" queried Freud. "You use the past tense, and yet you declare that he lives."

"I love him. Yes. That is much harder for me to say." She could feel the heat of her blush.

"This affectation causes you embarrassment?"

Eleanora felt a surge of anger accompanied by the urgent desire to depart. She always felt these two feelings in tandem. She stood up to leave, and then replied, "My affection is not an affectation, Dr. Freud, and yes, it causes me distress; because it is unrequited. But I see that you neither believe me nor understand me. And so, good day."

Freud did not rise, nor did he respond to her agitation in any way. Instead he continued the conversation in an even tone. "I think it is not affection of which you speak, Lady Ashburton, for the letter purporting to be from Mr. Wilde to yourself is certainly affectionate." He looked up, directly into her eyes, and said: "It is a passion, an uncontrollable, erotic passion. Is it not?"

Eleanora sank back down into her chair. "It is as you say, Dr. Freud."

"And yet you consult me in order to help this friend of yours, Mr. Oscar Wilde, and not yourself?"

"My feelings for him are a torment to me, it is true, but his feelings, his passions, why they have destroyed his entire life. If he is to live again, to have some happiness in this new time that he has been given, he must be cured; not only of his bodily illness, and of his melancholy, but of his…what you would call his…neurosis."

"Of his desire for men?"

"You speak of it so easily."

"I am not English. And it is a subject of much scientific interest to me. Sexual perversion is not a neurotic illness, Lady Ashburton, but its opposite."

"You think it is normal?"

"Not quite. Follow what I say. Normal neurotics, like you, and like me, live in a world of inner conflict. Our feelings are sometimes, as you put it, a torment to us. A man like Mr. Wilde found his torment in the world outside himself, a world that would not tolerate the kind of man that he knew himself to be. Even you who loved him could not accept this about him, no?"

Eleanora again felt the hot flush of emotion. It was a moment before she could compose herself. "Then you cannot cure him?"

"In regard to his love of men? No more than I could cure the world. I have not so much grandiosity. But I have read of your Mr. Wilde and I believe, had he come to me of his own free will, I could have helped him with another difficulty…his will to destroy himself. Now that is a neurotic compulsion, and psychoanalysis can certainly cure it. Unfortunately, people who wish to die seldom come for cures."

"Would you go to him?"

Freud paused, noting the strength of her belief system. He made a clinical decision. When he answered, he spoke from within its framework. "I see you do love him indeed, for I have told you I cannot make him yours and still you want me to help him. That is very admirable, Lady Ashburton, but as you are here, and I am here, and Mr. Wilde is not, perhaps we should turn our attention to curing you of the aspect of your love that is a torment to you."

Eleanora was amazed at the effrontery of this Austrian doctor who, in his own life, had managed to be both obscure and notorious at the same time. It was a pleasant amazement. Her years of friendship with Oscar had increased her enjoyment of effrontery.

"I have no wish to be cured, Dr. Freud."

Freud smiled softly. His gentle eyes sought her own. "You see what diffident creatures we are, Lady Ashburton? In matters of passion, we prefer our pain to our peace of mind."

"I fear I have taken up your precious time for nothing," she apologized, preparing herself to leave in an orderly fashion.

"Not at all. The puzzle with which you present me is most interesting. And the idea that Mr. Wilde is alive, most curious. If I may be so bold as to inquire, where is he to live, after he leaves the monastery, for certainly no island will hold a man of his energy for very long?"

"I have not yet formed a plan in such an event. Dear Oscar has always had religious leanings and we...that is I, hope that once he has made peace with the need for anonymity, he will adapt to the monastic life which has the peace of prison without its penury." She glanced again at Freud, with a defiant hope in her eyes. "Unless he came to me."

Freud had taken note of her slip: the use of the plural pronoun and her quick recovery. He deduced that someone else figured in her contrivances, probably a male helper. He nodded, hoping to encourage her narrative.

She continued. "Oscar Wilde's unjust confinement in the prisons of England, as terrible as it was, had a salutary effect on his writing, Dr. Freud. Perhaps you have read *The Ballad of Reading Gaol?*"

"I have heard of it, but not yet had the pleasure of its company."

"It is by far the best poem he has written; and an essay, sent as a letter to his lover Bosie Douglas from the gaol, is yet to be published, but it will support my assertion that he is a deeper, more mature artist since his imprisonment. A quiet life will, I hope, produce even finer work, for his talent is fierce. But if Oscar will not see reason and reside at the monastery, I suppose he will have to abide in Venice proper. It might be large enough to satisfy him."

Freud was listening to the story with a busy ear, collecting details for future contemplation and intervention. "Will he reappear as Oscar Wilde or Sebastian Melmoth?" he queried.

"Oh, he must remain hidden. He will need to adopt yet another name for the remainder of his writing life so that he may live and work without distractions; without being sought out by…the old temptations…by Lord Alfred Douglas. Bosie."

"He agrees to this?"

"What choice has he?"

"So, in Oscar's case, anonymity is destiny."

"Yes, I'm afraid so."

She was a most interesting woman, thought Freud. Sophisticated intelligence and imagination were at work in a highly unusual combination. He continued his attempts to draw her out. "Venice is a secretive city, a city of intrigue, that is part of its romance," he observed. "I am very fond of Venice. So unlikely a place to have been built at all, unless, of course, you understand the workings of the human mind."

"Pray, tell me what you mean, Dr. Freud."

It seemed he had only succeeded in drawing himself out. "Venice, like the mind, is a quite fantastic place and always under the threat of imminent submersion."

"Yes. Well. Thank you Dr. Freud." She simply had no idea how to evaluate this man with his bad beef and good servants and eccentric notions. She wanted to retreat to a private place and think about him for a time. She stood once more, and peered around the room uneasily.

This time, Freud also stood, and indicated a different door from the one through which she had entered.

"This arrangement allows for my patients to come and go in complete privacy," he explained. "Everyone has their secrets. Sometimes I am fortunate enough to be one of them."

Eleanora stepped outside the door and turned back suddenly, not knowing quite how to leave this strange, disappointing encounter with anything resembling her usual grace. "Thank you, again, Dr. Freud," she murmured, and extended her hand.

Freud took her hand. He bowed slightly, but did not release her. Instead he observed her closely, much too closely for her to be comfortable. Then, dropping her hand without warning, he unexpectedly renewed their conversation. "Here, here. Do not be so downcast, Lady Ashburton. Where there is love there is hope. No? How long will you be in Vienna?"

"I am uncertain. I am unhappy in England. Here I am the guest of Lord and Lady Caldwell-Allen who kindly say I may stay as long as I wish. It was the Caldwell-Allens who spoke in such a provocative manner about you, and of your unconventional ideas."

"And you are a woman who is drawn to men with unconventional ideas."

"You speak your mind about me, Dr. Freud."

"Yes. That is the idea exactly. Well. We have taken the measure of one another, have we not? Should you decide to return to me I think it would be best if you were to lie down on the couch. And come six days a week. I have an hour free at eleven each morning. Good day, then, Lady Ashburton. Please convey my regards to the Caldwell-Allens—if I am not another of your secret men."

CHAPTER 6

"I pray for your friend, Oscar," said Abate Antonio. "And I worry for him, Mr. Tyharde. He is far from God."

"But how can this be? Three years ago, on the very morning he was released from Reading Gaol, his first request to the world was to retreat from it. He asked to enter a Jesuit monastery. He asked for sanctuary. It was denied him, of course, and he wept. Surely he wouldn't have made this particular request if he didn't long for redemption."

"My cousins, the Jesuits, failed him with their refusal. I like to think my brothers, the Franciscans, would have been more understanding, for perhaps in that one moment his heart was completely open."

"These last three years of wandering around Europe, the rejections, the deaths, the gathering illness, the numberless boys—forgive me, Father—they have destroyed him as prison did not. Still, we who love him hope for a recovery. You understand my love is—"

"There, there, Timothy," interrupted the Abate. "May I call you Timothy? I only said that I worried for him." He laid a comforting hand on Timothy's shoulder. "Where there is worry, there is hope."

"Has he mentioned Bosie?"

"Lord Alfred Douglas? Yes, without remorse."

Timothy shook his head sadly. "And you counsel me to have hope?"

"I do. Consider Oscar Wilde and his lover with a larger mind. Though the Prince of Darkness took hold of their relationship and twisted it to his evil purposes, we must remember that God brought them together, for love was present between Oscar and Bosie. I think, perhaps it is still present. It could be years, a century, even a millennium before we can glimpse God's purposes in uniting these two men, but be assured that He has one."

Timothy was both comforted and confused by the Abate's words. He spoke from the Church's traditional position of intolerance when he spoke of evil, and yet he seemed to be counseling Christ's original tolerance in the same breath. He had liked Abate Antonio from the moment the cassocked man had stretched out his hand to guide Timothy from the rocking boat onto the gritty shore of the remote island.

"Would you like to see your friend now?"

"Yes. Yes, I am eager to see him."

"I will summon Fra Ricardo. He will take you to Mr. Wilde. Let us pray quietly until he arrives to escort you."

To Timothy, the son of a vicar, this was an easier idea than it would be to some men. After his brief prayer Timothy followed the kindly Fra Ricardo along the grey stone corridors. Except for the murmur of birds nesting in the rafters, silence prevailed. They halted before a heavy wooden door, one of many, and the monk smiled encouragingly. Timothy knocked quietly. There was a murmur of assent from within. Fra Ricardo turned away and Timothy tarried, listening to the slap of the friar's sandals, disappearing back into the silence of the cloister. Overhead a sea gull cried. Timothy opened the door and stepped into the cell.

Oscar was seated before the fire toasting some bread on a poker held over the flames. A peacock stood expectantly beside his chair. A parrot sat on his shoulder. "Just a moment, Fra Ricardo," said Oscar, not looking up, "I am about my domestic duties."

Timothy stood quietly, watching his kind friend without interruption. To Timothy's eyes Oscar's complexion appeared healthy, though his form was obscured by a monk's cassock.

Oscar finished toasting the bread, blew on it gently to cool it, and then offered half to the peacock, half to the parrot. All three appeared satisfied. Oscar then looked up from his tasks and a smile of pure delight overcame his features at the sight of Timothy, who felt as if he, too, had been given perfectly toasted golden bread.

"Greetings, my dear Tim," said Oscar, lifting a nearby cup in salute, "what brings you to the Lagoon?"

"Oh pleasure, pleasure, what brings one anywhere?" replied Timothy with an answering smile. "The pleasure of seeing you, Oscar. And in apparent good health and spirits at last."

"Oh, the friars here are fierce physicians, I assure you. When it comes to healing, that plump Fra Ricardo has a genuine satanic gift. But I must be ever alert. They want my soul in exchange."

"Yes. I hear you are quite unrepentant."

Oscar laughed. "How delightful! You've been listening to gossip. I didn't know they had gossip here. Gossip is the only truth that has any measurable effect on one's life. Have some wine."

Timothy's smile gave way to laughter. "It is wonderful to laugh with you again, Oscar. You are truly back from the dead, are you not?"

"I know it is to you and Eleanora that I owe this macabre reincarnation. How do you like my cassock? Do I look like Balzac? Tell the truth now. The best mirror is an old friend."

"It gives you an entirely new grandeur," pronounced Timothy. "Here it is wise to let the birds display the more ostentatious plumages." He scooted the peacock out of the room where it stalked into the square of sunlight in the center of the cloister.

"Be a good bird," admonished Oscar, "or James Whistler will come and make a cartoon of you."

Chuckling, Oscar shut the door. "Do you remember, Tim, how Whistler lost his richest patron by painting the man's drawing room wall with a huge cartoon of a poor peacock being killed by a rich one?"

"I had heard the story."

"Whatever were we all doing in those days, we esthetes?"

"Having a bit of fun?" suggested Timothy.

"Like common Cockneys? Oh, there was more to it than that surely. We quested for beauty, for art, for grandeur." He shrugged his shoulders. "Albeit with a bit of fun."

He lifted the parrot to a perch near the fireplace. "I call him Hector, which he does very well. I'm sure he has another appellation, a good Italian one, but he hasn't told me what it is, and seems to take no offence at being addressed as Hector. The Franciscans here have quite an aviary. They talk to all the birds—you wouldn't think that talking to birds could become religious dogma, but it has—however, this bird talks to me." He put another crumb of toast upon the perch.

"Grazie," said the parrot.

"Prego," said Oscar.

"Charming," said Timothy. "Now Oscar, I've a small speech to make, will you hear me out?"

"Of course, dear Tim. For months I've heard only birds, bells, and brothers. It will be lovely to listen to a good British pronouncement. The subject is unimportant." He settled into his chair, and looked up at Tim expectantly.

"I've come to convey my regard for you and to tell you that Lady Eleanora and Auguste Rodin also send their love. They are the only people, besides the brothers here, who know that you live. Your other friends, Robbie, Reggie, the lot...are quite stricken with grief. In your absence they have been reaching out to one another, becoming closer."

"How touching. Like the spindly trees in a forest stretching out their branches over a fallen oak."

"They are riddled with guilt," continued Timothy.

"The worms of Conscience gnawing at their pith. Rightly so."

"The world is not the same without you."

"This I could have told the world. I believe I did," he added with a weary sigh.

"Do let me continue, Oscar," pressed Timothy.

"Carry on, my dear man."

"As you have doubtless surmised, it is Lady Eleanora who supplies the money for this adventure. The friars here accept only a small donation—they think of you as a holy mission—which I suppose is how Eleanora thinks of you, too, but there have been, and will be, other expenses, not the least of them Rodin's fee for your effigy. He would have done it without payment, but Eleanora insisted."

"A fine woman, our Eleanora. Not, thankfully a good woman, or I would be dead, you would be shivering in some British idea of spring, and Auguste Rodin would have a good deal less silver in his pocket."

"Your in-laws continue to support your sons, of course. I have it on good account that the boys are doing well in their newest school, wherever that may be. Both Cyril and Vyvyan believe, of course, that you are dead, and have suffered most terribly on that account. It is the one great fault to our plot, their sorrow so unrelieved. But they are resilient boys. And full of the enthusiasms of youth."

Oscar looked as if had been struck. All signs of pleasure faded from his features. He turned away and stared hard at the fire, fighting to keep his composure. Timothy, always awkward in the face of Oscar's strong emotions, stood quietly, too reserved to continue.

It was Oscar who broke the silence, his voice gentle. "I used to believe that there were two worlds—an adult's world and a child's world; and that with the exercise of discretion these two spheres could be kept apart, as safe from one another's influence as are the celestial bodies hurtling through the infinity of night. But it is not so. Shadows fall across the moon. Meteors strike the earth. Worlds collide. My adult world smashed into my sons' fragile planet with enough force to shatter us all."

Timothy, unschooled in any alternative response, said simply, "I'm sorry, Oscar."

"Am I never to see them again? My sons."

"I know not, Oscar."

"And am I to live on here alone, a breathing corpse in this dank stone tomb? Why not take me to San Michele and have done with the charade?"

Timothy shuddered. He had passed the Isola de San Michele, the Venetians' cemetery island, on his journey across the lagoon, its high, stone walls enclosing only the dead. "That is not a thing to say to a friend, Oscar," he reprimanded.

"The Chinese are quite correct when they refuse to save a drowning man. They know that by custom they will be responsible for the man's life thereafter, and they know, too, that the chances of his being a perfect fool are quite high or he wouldn't have been drowning in the first place."

"Well, you are not a fool, and I would rather take responsibility for you than bury you."

"I suppose it would appear churlish of me anyway—to be buried in two cemeteries at one time." Oscar managed a weak smile at his companion, which allowed Timothy to relax a little. Oscar began to toast another slice of bread.

"I must disturb you with one bit of bad news, Oscar. I thought you should hear it from a friend."

"Who else has died?" queried Oscar in an even voice, without looking away from the fire, but Timothy saw his shoulders tense. This man who had lost so much, knew he was about to sustain another loss.

"Queen Victoria."

Oscar rose abruptly; his bread fell to the hearth unheeded. He stood unsteadily, his hand on his heart. He looked both shocked and saddened. "Long live the King," he said, then added, in a voice Timothy knew to be sincere: "I loved our dear little Queen. I think she was the only woman to whom I might have been happily married."

"I knew of your affection for her, Oscar, though I cannot say I fully understand it. Her ideas of morality seemed entirely at odds with your own tastes, and she signed that dreadful law that put you into prison."

"She acted, always, according to her nature. That is the thing. Her morality came from within her; so she lived it and wore it and ate it and drank it and signed it. I admired her greatly for she succeeded, in spite of all the pressures of her high position, even above being a queen, in being herself. She was, like me, an original, though not so well dressed. Were you in England at the time?"

"Yes. I was in Portsmouth in February to look at some fine porcelain pieces, newly arrived from China. I went out to the harbor, of course, to see the great sight as her body was brought back from the Isle of Wight."

"Escorted by massive battleships?"

"All the ships in harbor sounded their cannons and the sunset turned grey with smoke. It was beautiful and sad, and very noisome."

"I have outlived the Queen. I never thought to do so. What new age comes upon us, Timothy?"

"Pane," reminded Hector.

Oscar sat down again and retrieved the fallen toast, and lifted it up to the parrot, thinking his own thoughts for a while before brightening and looking over at Timothy. "By the way," he asked, reaching for another piece of bread, "how was my funeral?"

"What a peculiar question," said Timothy, startled by the query. After a moment's pause, he replied: "Quite the proper thing, I reckon." He settled himself near to Oscar who was again busy at his fireside task. The peasant bread sent up a delicious aroma as the fire did its handiwork.

"All funerals are proper," declared Oscar. "That is what funerals are for. Why without funerals one would never have the opportunity to demonstrate the full extent of one's hypocrisy. But I want to know the details. You must tell me everything. I don't expect to have this chance again. Tell me of the eulogies."

Oscar crossed his long legs, and bit into his own nicely browned toast with a satisfying crunch. The eyes of the parrot opened wide with interest. Oscar looked at Tim with an equivalent expectancy. "There weren't any eulogies. Everyone was struck dumb by the loss of you."

"Paralyzed by the fear of public opinion, more like."

"But you were done well by. The funeral was in the Church of Saint-Germaine-des-Prés. It's the oldest cathedral in Paris, you know."

"Of course I know. But it's decorated with those awful frescoes."

"The sanctuary is otherwise pleasant."

"Narrow."

"That couldn't be helped, Oscar."

"I suppose not," he conceded grumpily.

"Because you made a deathbed conversion there was a requiem Mass. The priest managed everything very well as far as I could tell, not being a Catholic myself."

"How many were in attendance?"

"I counted fifty-six."

"Not my largest house." Oscar said this lightly, but Timothy detected that the small number stung him.

"But with the exception of the journalists, everyone present was most sincere in their devotion to you."

"Quite the opposite, old boy, the journalists were most sincere in their grief. I was bread and butter to them."

Timothy decided not to discuss journalists with his friend. The popular press was a subject that evoked Oscar's most terrible passions. Instead, he carried on: "And there were quite a lot of flowers—"

Oscar brightened. "Lilies?"

"From Robbie, but it was chrysanthemums for the most part, I'm afraid, given the time of year."

"Next time I must remember to die in the spring."

"And there were two rather awful beaded wreaths from the hotel proprietor, Dupoirier, and his hotel staff. These wreaths appear indestructible, and will doubtless outlast us all."

"Dear Dupoirier. What a blessing he was to me in those final months. Waited on me hand and foot, never asked a penny of me. And Bosie?"

There, thought Timothy. The name's been said and the island hasn't sunk beneath the waves. He replied cautiously. "Bosie was there, of course. He paid for everything. He arrived as swiftly after you…after you died as he could, from Scotland. He was in a perfect pet at not being allowed to see your body."

"How peculiar. The sight of my body was never a cause célèbre for dear Bosie. It was quite the other way around, I assure you."

Timothy blanched. "Oscar, I say."

Oscar preoccupied, appeared not to notice Timothy's discomfiture. "Why *wasn't* he there sooner? I should have liked to expire in his sinuous arms."

"He complained that no one had informed him of your approach to death's door."

"Why wasn't he told?"

"Your love of Bosie Douglas doesn't make him lovable to any one else. No one else wanted him about. To be perfectly frank, Oscar, it is just as well. Bosie's presence would have made our plans to save you quite impossible."

"That, to be sure, is Bosie's raison d'être. How furious he would be to know he had paid for a faux funeral, but he is always furious at one thing or another so I suppose it doesn't matter what particular thing it is, actually. That evil Douglas temperament is a curse on him, Tim, a curse."

"Bosie. So you will continue to worry yourself about Bosie after everything?"

"All men love the thing that kills them."

"Why not let Bosie go, Oscar, into the past? Start anew."

"I take a fair amount of pride in my loyalties," Oscar remonstrated. "I believe that to abandon my affection for Bosie would be to die for a fourth time."

"Fourth?" asked Timothy, more curious than chastened.

"The first was in prison when, for a short time, and for the only time in my life, I blamed and hated others for my misfortunes. That was the death of my self-respect. The second death was a few months after my release, when I lived again with Bosie in Naples and knew my burning passion for him had been damped down to the lowest flame of friendship. That was the death of passion; by far the worst. The third was in that wretched hotel room in Paris. You were there, Tim. You saw. I had let go of life. I was ready to die, and instead I've been given a vacation in Italy."

He still has his talent, thought Timothy. "I do wish you would write again, Oscar."

"Here in this monastery? Oh for a muse of friars?" He handed Tim some toasted bread. "Have some toast."

"Then you must decide how you wish to live. Choose with care, Oscar, for our fates, Lady Eleanora's and mine, are now bound up with yours. I will endeavor to make any arrangements that seem feasible."

"Feasible?" Oscar stood up in apparent agitation. "I have never in my life been feasible!"

"Reasonable then," countered Timothy.

"Reasonable to whom, Tim? I fear a small apartment near the Roman Colosseum equipped with a steady supply of beautiful young men will not seem reasonable to you in the least. I fear a quaint villa in Malta where I might live with Bosie in a modicum of comfort will also strike you as entirely unreasonable. I expect a fine hotel room with a good view in Bavaria is unreasonable, too?"

"Bavaria?"

"My boys' uncle, their guardian, lives in Bavaria. I might at least glimpse the boys again if I went there."

"What you wish for is not…reasonable."

"As I thought."

"Oscar, be sane. If Cyril and Vyvyan were to recognize you we'd have a first rate scandal on our hands."

"Well, we wouldn't want that, would we? Certainly a man in my position can ill afford a scandal!" He resumed his chair, crossed his arms, and adopted an obstinate look.

"What would it accomplish? You would doubtless frighten and confuse the boys and just when they seem to be adjusting, finally, after all their losses."

Oscar, who had been warmed with the thought of reunion, now felt the chill of his own demise fall across his heart. He paled and began to tremble. Timothy, poking at the fire as he argued, did not see the change in Oscar, nor hear him when he whispered: "They would have their father."

"And the boys' uncle would doubtless move them to another place, and that would constitute yet another disruption for them; and he would issue a restraining order on you, if not worse."

"Enough, Tim! Enough!" Oscar had raised his hand against the onslaught of words as if fending off physical blows.

Timothy, looking up from the fireside to his friend, was shocked at what he saw. "Oscar, what has come over you? Are you taken ill again?"

"This sudden palsy you see is the result of all I have endured. It comes over me when my mind is agitated. It is quite appalling. A man like myself quivering like a calf's foot jelly!"

"I'll fetch you the coverlet."

"No. Bring me the heavy cloak by the door."

Timothy hastily retrieved the sackcloth garment and helped Oscar wrap it around his shaking form. Timothy, now sunken into guilt, sat silently watching his friend who was trying to bring his trembling under control.

"You know, I sometimes think my eternal punishment will be that every epigram I ever wrote will come back to haunt me. Remember the line in *An Ideal Husband?* 'Fathers should be neither seen nor heard. That is the only proper basis for family life.'"

"I'm so sorry, Oscar."

"It's all right, Timothy. I know you have the well-being of my sons at heart." He smiled. "I shall behave myself. I'm too poor to do anything else."

"I'm on my way to Vienna to meet with Eleanora. I had hoped to take her the news that you were content on this island, but that is not to be. Can you cultivate patience for a short time while we work things out?"

"Is it not enough to have Prudence? Now I'm to be saddled with Patience as well?"

"Prudence!" said Hector with what sounded like genuine alarm.

"Now look what you've done," remonstrated Oscar, "Hector has attacks of anxiety at the allusion to any virtue in any language whatever. You see? His poor feathers are all ruffled. You understand why he prefers my company to that of the brothers. Well, I will try to be quick about it, and cultivate Patience."

He and the bird eyed each other for an uneasy moment.

"Now be a good fellow, Tim, and rush back to Venice proper and then off to Vienna by the night train from Mestre, and fix things up with Lady Eleanora. I'll need rooms in a city of reasonable charm and a modest allowance; or, as unlikely as it sounds, I shall be forced to live by my wits."

"It is not your wit that we fear, Oscar," replied Timothy with a small bow. "You shall have your way."

"It's the only thing worth having, Timothy. Oh, and Tim, one last favor?" Oscar stood up again and removed the cloak. He folded it and handed it to Timothy, who saw that Oscar's trembling had diminished. "You see, at the mention of liberation, I am quite recovered." Then in a stage whisper he asked if Timothy could have a decent lining sewn into the garment. "Some Venetian cut velvet would be divine; blue, I think, so soft against the skin; warm, but not too warm. These holy men out here have the skin of lizards."

The two men, having come to an understanding, shook hands warmly and took leave of one another and after saying goodbye to the Abate,

Timothy climbed into the gondola that had carried him to the island refuge. He told the boatman to return to Venice, but to make a stop at the island of Burano along the way. He had decided to buy Eleanora some lace. The errand would break the long watery passage across the lagoon, and the gift would please her in a way his news would not. This decision gave Oscar just the advantage over his friend that he needed.

CHAPTER 7

"A letter has come for you," said Lady Caldwell-Allen to Lady Eleanora Ashburton. "I saw it on the tray in the entrance hall this morning. Shall I ring for Hargrove?"

Eleanora paled. "Yes. Please. Was it from Italy? Did you notice?" she asked, keeping her voice as normal as possible.

"I couldn't say, my Dear," replied her imposing hostess. "Especially if I had been indiscreet enough to notice."

Both women smiled at the remark, but not at each other. Lady Caldwell-Allen never smiled except upon herself, and Eleanora's smile was one of recognition, for she had heard Oscar say the line, with a far superior delivery, years ago at a country weekend house party.

Lady Caldwell-Allen had once been a professional beauty in court circles, and was now aging into stout unattractiveness as a wealthy diplomat's wife in Vienna. Languidly—for she could still move her arms gracefully—she pulled the tasseled cord near her settee.

Hargrove, a butler of middle years and ancient reserve, arrived without pause and without haste.

"Would you bring in the letter that arrived for Lady Ashburton this morning?"

"Yes, your Ladyship."

"Thank you, Hargrove."

Eleanora, who had wanted to bolt from the drawing room and run out to the hall table upon hearing of the letter, sat quietly and stabbed at her needlework. She damned the manners of the upper classes that held her in her chair. "How very stupid smart people are," she thought.

"Did you ever visit the notorious Dr. Freud?" Lady Caldwell-Allen asked.

"I did indeed," she replied, pulling on a silken thread.

"What was he like? Did he agree to see your mysterious friend? I don't know where you manage to collect your men, Eleanora. You know that one cannot be too careful while in foreign parts. And this Dr. Freud... they say his methods for madness are quite revolutionary."

Eleanora knew that Lady Caldwell-Allen was torn between her desire to hear of her friend's adventure and her marked preference to do all the talking in any situation. Eleanora took a sip of tea before undertaking to satisfy the curiosity. Her own mind was turbulent; since hearing of the letter's arrival her thoughts were washing back and forth between the shores of wishes and the shoals of fear. Lady Caldwell-Allen was an annoying buzz in the room, but one to which she must attend. Eleanora set down her teacup and looked up from her embroidery. "Dr. Freud felt that I, not my friend, was in need of his treatments."

"What effrontery!" exclaimed her companion. "But it was to be expected, my dear, his pocket is in need of your good English pounds."

"Well, he—"

"And to sit with you in a darkened parlor discussing all that is unmentionable would, doubtless, give the doctor a great deal of less than proper pleasure. What kind of world are we coming to when we must pay money to talk of our misfortunes?"

Eleanora was spared the need to answer, for Hargrove reappeared with a silver tray in hand. Eleanora took the letter from the tray. It had no return address on the envelope, so she tore it open hastily.

"Is it from that Timothy fellow?" asked Lady Caldwell-Allen, not really caring one way or the other, but acting as if she did. "I don't know what you see in that young man. He is too, too...busy with other young men to spare much thought of you, my dear. But of course he is a great advance over Oscar Wilde. Whatever did we see in that horrid man, Eleanora?"

"We saw a man who never said a bad word about anyone," replied Eleanora, pointedly. Lady Caldwell-Allen stared at her blankly. "And one whose sheer delight in living, whose happiness, was infectious."

"Quite," replied her hostess, closing the subject with a sniff. "Your letter?"

"As it happens, it's from—" she broke off suddenly, realizing how closely she had come to revealing her dreadful, wonderful secret.

"From whom, did you say?"

"From my Aunt Gruzella, Lady Raines."

"Ah, yes. Well. I shall leave you to your letter then," said Lady Caldwell-Allen, arising with enough majesty to distract any onlooker from the onset of her early arthritis. "If you write to dear Lady Raines in reply, please convey my regards."

That would not take much ink, thought Eleanora. "Good afternoon," she said. "I shall see you at dinner."

At last she was alone with her letter.

My kindest and most courageous Eleanora,

Her hands had gone cold.

You are the strongest flower in the windswept garden of my life.

Oh, who could resist this man? She thought.

So it is through your good graces that I have come to watery Venice, instead of to my stony grave.

Tim must have told him everything!

I write to you now, my savior, from my palazzo, for I could bear a monkish cell no longer.

Eleanora felt her heart lurch. What did this mean?

From the window, which, in a most daring manner, I have opened a full inch, I can peep across the water to the Palazzo Alessandro.

"My God!" Eleanora exclaimed aloud. Recovering herself, her thoughts raced silently; he has escaped the Isola Francesco del Deserto. He is in Venice itself, and on the Grand Canal, no less! Oh, that is just like him.

> *The palazzo in which I reside is great heap of stone if one looks on it in shadow, but appears a magnificent confection in the sunlight. It took a great deal of cajoling to induce Tim to arrange this suite of rooms for me from an old and noble family which is to say, cash poor—a situation with which I feel enormous sympathy in my present circumstances. (You can indeed take "it" with you, I have found out, but "it," in my case, is nothing but a long list of debts!) You and Tim have done so much for me already! Still, I prevailed using the entire monthly allowance Timothy says you have granted me. Do not worry, I shall live on bread and water.*

Tim never stood a chance in an argument with Oscar. No one did. She smiled. This explained the urgent cable from Tim of the previous week asking for a larger monthly allowance.

> *The Abate Antonio has promised to keep my cell in readiness and I plan to visit it occasionally, for on that remote island I can walk about freely whereas here I must keep to these rooms and a small back garden, and the garden only in the dark of night when the flowers smell like delicious poisons, and the moon among the chimneys casts only dreadful black shapes to creep along the graveled paths amidst its silver light. I am, nevertheless, rapturous to breathe and walk and to do the simplest things I would never have even noticed before my fall from grace. Is that too grand? Too biblical? Nothing was ever too grand for me, nor I too grand for it, before my unfortunate demise in Paris. But now a choppy patch of murky green water, glimpsed from my narrow window, is to be my meager slice of life, and with which I must make do until…until when, my jewel, my prism? What is to become of me? Am I to remain hidden forever? To what purpose?*

"To love me," replied Eleanora spontaneously. She hadn't meant to speak aloud again, and certainly not of this most secret of desires. She shook her head as if to shake loose the notion. One's own mind is shameless, she observed, it will think anything! She watched the comings and goings of her mind more closely now, since the meeting with Freud.

> *Tim seems not to have thought very far ahead. He wanted only for me to recover and to live and to write again. But how can I write if I am completely cut off from society? What am I to write of? Green water, moonlight and shadow take but a short while to describe. Then what? I know it is your money that cares for me. How am I to repay you? Eleanora, you have always been smarter than any man. Reply. Reply in haste. I shall not breathe until I hear from you. Send by way of the Abate. A monk attends me and will bring me your letter. My kindest love, my deepest gratitude, my impatient eagerness…I am signed Sebastian, only to safeguard our delicious secret.*

Eleanora sat for a long time with the letter on her lap, then she rang for Hargrove and requested writing instruments.

She did not, however, write to Oscar.

CHAPTER 8

"How in God's name did he get all the way into Venice, Timothy? Did he steal a boat?"

Lady Eleanora Ashburton and Timothy Tyharde were seated in the Café Lalo, near the Cathedral. Steaming bowls of hot rich chocolate had been placed before them, fortification against unusually cold late spring weather.

"He swam."

"In April? In his condition? It's miles across the lagoon. He couldn't have done."

"He has always had the constitution of a dray horse. He used to swim those cold Irish lakes as a boy. The lagoon must have seemed a mud puddle by comparison."

"Where did you find him? What did he say?" demanded Eleanora.

"He sent a boy to meet my gondola at the Fondamenta Nuova. He had swum a short cut round the back of Burano where I had stopped to buy your lace and beaten me to Venice by a full half-hour. I found him comfortably warm and dry, seated before a brick oven in a fish restaurant near the Gesuati church. A workman along the dock had loaned him some rain gear to cover himself, and he had cleverly fooled me into bringing his cloak along in my gondola. The locals thought he was a mad monk."

"Well, they were half right, weren't they? What did he say?"

"He informed me that the lagoon fish were excellent in character, he had gotten to know them intimately during his swim; in taste they were not quite so excellent as the rascasse, the coastal rock fish necessary to the perfection of French bouillabaisse, but nevertheless they had their own distinction; and if I wasn't in the mood for fish, I should have to make do with pasta."

"What did you do?"

"I ate the fish. It was superb."

"Timothy, I meant what did you do with Oscar?"

"But you know perfectly well what I did. He cajoled me into the rooms at the Palazzo Contarini; said he should perish if I returned him to the Isola Francesco del Deserto; swore he would write plays and poetry again in civilized surroundings. What should I have done? He's bigger than me by half. I could hardly take him back by force."

"Yes. Yes. You have done all that could be done." Eleanora stirred her chocolate and drank the entire cup down in one draught, letting the sweetness flood her system. "Did anyone see you? Did anyone recognize him?"

"You would have read all about it in the newspapers if he had been recognized. No. He wears his monkish garb as if he were born to it. And Eleanora—"

"Yes?"

"Without access to his bottle of Koko Maricopas his hair is completely white, a rather beautiful silvery white with no grey to it. And his teeth, so blackened by the bad poor medical care in his youth, they have also been restored as white as pearls. Heaven knows what the monks have been giving him. And his gauntness creates a natural disguise. He appears to be a tall, old, deeply religious man. Not Oscar Wilde at all. One of those ancient Italian women, all in black, crossed herself when she saw him. He loved that, of course. He seemed quite content when I left him in the Palazzo. The rooms are furnished with beautiful, if slightly beaten-up, antiques; the maid is attentive; the food good; and there's the small courtyard garden hidden away in the back for fresh air."

"Yes. He mentioned the garden in his letter. He both revels in it and reviles it, as his place of freedom and confinement."

"Fra Ricardo rows in once or twice a week to check on his health, and the Abate arrives on Monday evenings to converse with him. It's against the protocol of the monastery, of course, but when did normal rules ever apply in Oscar's circle?"

"We testify to that," mused Eleanora. "I think he has a way of releasing everything he touches from the bonds of conformity, whether for good or ill."

"Sometimes Fra Ricardo brings a parrot. Oscar befriended the creature on the Isola, and Franciscans are serious about birds. So Fra Ricardo rows him into Venice for visits. It is quite a sight, the rainbow of plumage sitting haughtily on the shoulder of the humble brown monk. Hector, Oscar calls it, though I discovered its real name is Giancarlo."

"At least he doesn't call it Bosie. Well, by his letter you can see that he has become restless rather quickly, parrot or no parrot."

"He carries his prison experience with him. Everything feels like a gaol to him."

"Well, everything is. What do you think he will do, Tim?"

Timothy shrugged his shoulders. "Oscar is, to use a well worn phrase, a loose cannon."

"He would make it fresh...he would call himself 'a loose canon,' spelled with a single *n*."

Tim smiled. "I don't think there is any keeping him. He will swim the Adriatic next, I suppose, or climb across the Alps. He wants to see his sons."

"And Bosie Douglas?" She asked what she was afraid to ask.

Timothy, who knew Eleanora well enough to have intuited her passion for Oscar, replied as gently as he could. "He claims only a friendship with Bosie now. But yes, he wants to see him."

"Well, he can't, and that is that!" she exclaimed. "I have to put my foot down somewhere. If I'm to support him, he must behave himself."

"You sound exactly like his wife."

"Oh do be quiet, Tim!" Eleanora had regretted her outburst immediately.

Timothy sipped at his chocolate. He watched as she slowly recovered her equanimity. Eleanora had disliked Constance, Oscar's wife, on first acquaintance and the aversion had deepened over time. She had found

Constance insipid, ill-matched to a man of genius, naive, and finally, willfully blind. Eleanora had not forgiven Constance, even in death, for her treatment of Oscar subsequent to his release from Reading Gaol. Constance had kept herself and their sons from Oscar at the time he most needed his family. She had suffered greatly from the scandal, of course, but had she not been so shallow she would have made something of her trauma, forged a brave new life with her poet husband. Instead she hid away under a false name, took every kind of bad advice from her family, and by her absence, all but pushed Oscar back into Bosie's bed.

"Can you forget I ever said that, about the conditions on the money?" she asked.

"If you can forget my reply."

"Done. I will go to Venice and see him."

He leaned back in the cushioned chair, relieved. "When will you go?"

"Sunday. The night train."

"Good. That's settled then. Let's go some place where we can get a real drink. Oscar says the only good time to drink is before lunch."

"I can't, Tim. It's gone eleven and I'm already late for another appointment."

"Where are you off to? Can I escort you?"

Eleanora appeared startled by his quite ordinary offer. Flustered, she paused before answering, as she hurriedly pulled on her gloves. "No, Timothy. I'm fine on my own. I'm off to my dressmaker. It isn't far."

Her manner puzzled Timothy. Eleanora flushed and left quickly with a falsely cheerful wave of the hand. He felt for the first time in all the years that he had known Eleanora that she had not spoken the truth to him, but instead was keeping some secret here in Vienna. Could she at last have taken a lover? Would it free her from her obsession with Oscar? He wondered as the door closed swiftly behind her, then he leaned forward and stared into the dregs of his chocolate. He was suddenly sick to death of secrets.

CHAPTER 9

O scar Wilde paced restlessly, at the edge of the sea. From time to time he glared at the clear expanse of green water. Other seas are blue, he thought, but the Adriatic is a most tiresome green. Why, he wondered, was the world the way it was and not some other way?

His cassock rustled in the gentle wind from the sea. He knew he wouldn't be recognized, even on this popular beach, defaced as it was with so many Englishmen. His sackcloth made a monk of him, his trim white beard hid his large, recognizable chin, and the little bald spot he shaved on the top of his head was the finishing touch. It had required bravado to put razor to pate, but it had assured his solitude.

He did not want to be on the Lido. He wanted to be in Paris. He wanted to go by way of Heidelberg, where he imagined his sons might be enjoying their summer holidays with his former in-laws, if enjoyment could be found among such rigid old sticks. He would go wearing his monk disguise as in a fairy story.

The children had once loved the fairy stories he had written for them. Oscar sighed. The stories he had bequeathed them were a mixed lot, the ones he had written himself were delightful; but the last one, written by the British journalists, was soul-destroying. Had his dear sons read that disgraceful story of Oscar Wilde as yet? The newspapers had been hidden from them at the time of his trials. Constance had assured him that the boys knew nothing of the scandal. But how long can the truth of one's father be kept from the curious mind of a child?

Oscar and his elder brother, Willie, had been raised in Dublin along-side his father's collection of illegitimate children. "His other family," his mother, Speranza, had called them. She held herself to be above common scandal, though when his father was accused of molesting a female patient, Oscar and Willie were taken from their home in Merrion Square to a fashionable seaside resort in an ineffectual attempt to shield them from their papa's notoriety and the libel suit that arose from his misdeeds. His mother had been unbroken. Years later, Oscar's wife had collapsed in shame.

"What have you done, Oscar," she had cried out to him, "what have you done?" And she had fled from England with his sons.

He would go to them again, his darling Cyril, his adoring Vyvyan. Yes, he thought, he would go as a wandering holy man, though the Germans would think him mad—rather a compliment in Germany, he mused. Cyril would be sixteen now, almost the age of the young men that he had…he discontinued the thought. Vyvyan would be fourteen. The children he had known were gone forever. He would never see his laughing, loving, little boys again.

Perhaps I should just swim out and out and out until I drown, he thought, for there must be some limit to even my endurance. He took a tentative step into the water to test the idea. Across the narrow sea lay the Balkans. It would be just his luck to make it all the way across. He didn't want to go to the Balkans, of that he was quite certain. Mad, the Slovaks, the Serbs, and the Croats, endlessly killing one another in revenge of ancient dead relatives they most likely would have loathed if they had actually known them.

Just then, out of the corner of his eye, he caught sight of a woman billowing rapidly towards him along the beach. She was not dressed for bathing, but in fashionable apparel of the same cowslip color as his wife's wedding dress—the one he had designed for her. The phantom made straight for him, approaching, like a great fluttering ghost across the sands.

Fear overtook him, for surely this was his wife who approached with such determination; but Constance was dead. He had taken flowers and wept upon her grave before going off with that fetching young Italian boy for the weekend. Was this the soul of Constance then, coming nigh to berate him? I am officially dead, he thought, no one has the right to haunt me. As she came closer she looked less and less like a ghost and more and more like a very determined woman—a thing far more frightening than any perturbed spirit! Then a terrible idea assailed him: perhaps neither of them was dead. Perhaps, Constance had been spirited away somewhere by wrong-headed, well-meaning friends as well, all in the service of this ridiculous seaside reunion.

She had nearly reached him when he recognized the woman.

He sank to his knees in relief.

"Oscar, Dear Oscar." Lady Ashburton was saying as she planted a kiss directly on his bald spot.

"Eleanora, my savior," he cried. "You see me here, the effect of your cause. I once said I would never live to see the new century; I was sure that the English would not stand for it. But you, my rescuing angel, have returned the century to me, and the English be damned." He saw that she was weeping.

He was about to kiss the hem of her garment when Prudence intervened: she was whispering to him, warning him to be careful, telling him that this woman was in love with him. This couldn't be, he thought loudly in contradiction, for she is only my dear friend, Eleanora, my Swan, my companion of so many years. Prudence was persistent, opening his eyes to an old reality that he had not seen until this moment: Lady Eleanora had always loved him. He must act with caution, and with Prudence, for it was to Eleanora that he owed his life and, of more pressing concern, his keep.

Oscar arose brushing the sand from his robes while composing himself. He smiled and took hold of her arm as he had done so often in happier days.

"We must walk arm and arm for a time along the sands thereof," he suggested, and they began a slow, calm perambulation enjoying the togetherness of old friends, now both embittered and sweetened for Oscar with his new awareness of her passion. "I thought for a moment that you were Constance," he confided.

Eleanora dried her tears on an elaborate lace handkerchief. What, she was wondering, had he ever seen in the vexatious Constance? She had been hopelessly inadequate to her husband's needs, until her own abrupt finale under the knife. Anyone who would submit to spinal surgery in Italy could not be altogether bright, thought Eleanora, without mercy. To Oscar she said only, "that must have been a shock to your mind."

"Everything shocks me nowadays," he replied, stepping gingerly away from a wavelet. "My mind has become quite unbalanced by clean living. Why just the other evening a tourist in the Piazza San Marco shocked me simply by staring at me."

"You go to such crowded places?" Eleanora questioned. "Whatever will we all do if you are recognized?"

"For a moment, as I sat at Florian's, with a cognac in my hand and a pigeon on my shoulder, I thought I was indeed found out. I said, 'Why are you staring at me, Sir?' And do you know what was his reply?"

"I don't dare to think."

"He said: 'Pardon me, Father, but you bear a striking resemblance to an English writer, a Mr. George Bernard Shaw. He has hair like yours and a beard cut so, though perhaps he is not as white as you. He, too, wears a downcast expression. I am sorry to intrude on your meditation...' he said, noticing the cognac mid-sentence. The cheeky fellow was about to turn away, but I could not stand it, Eleanora; I could not stand to hear him mistaken in so horrid a fashion, so I blurted out the truth."

"Oh, Oscar, no!"

"I did, so help me to heaven, I did. I leaned forward across the little white table and looked him square in the face and I said, 'Young man, Mr. George Bernard Shaw is an *Irish* writer.'" With this Oscar gave out with a great guffaw of laughter and Eleanora, relieved, laughed with him. He continued, "I did not say that Mr. Shaw was very short and rather less attractive than I am, because that would have been unkind."

"Timothy told me you were in poor spirits, Oscar, but I find you well."

"I am well enough Eleanora for a dead man, but I must go back to Paris, and I have no means of conveyance. A hearse will not travel so far, I reckon."

"But why Paris, Oscar? Why not content yourself awhile in Venice?"

"The whole place reminds me of Ruskin, my old Oxford don. It's as if by writing about Venice so well he has carved his name into the very stones of the city. And Ruskin reminds me of England, and all that was, and when I close my eyes and think of England I fall back into the most hateful melancholy."

"But this is a fancy, Oscar. Can you not be happy as you are? To be in good health, and loved by many, known by few, and living in a beautiful city?"

"It is what everyone of maturity desires, isn't it? And few experiences in life so mature a man as the survival of his own demise, yet—"

"And to have the time to write. In that, you should take happiness."

"But Eleanora—"

"And to know that your children are well and lovingly cared for, in that you should be happy—"

"There, there, dear Eleanora. You are far too young and far too beautiful to play the encouraging Friar Lawrence to my despondent Romeo."

"But I so wanted—"

"By now you must know that no one ever gets what is wanted from life."

He patted her arm gently. Her face changed. Oscar watched as sadness arrived, first in the set of her features, then in the glittering of her eyes. He felt a responsibility to lighten the mood. Suddenly he realized that he had felt a need to lighten the mood of the entire world for his whole life. Briefly he wondered how and where this had begun. Perhaps it had been when his father lay dying in an upstairs bedroom in their home on Merrion Square. Each morning a woman in black, heavily veiled, had arrived at the house, and unimpeded by his mother or her servants, climbed the stairs where she sat silently at his bedside, the other mother of the other family. Was his mother noble to allow it, or was she a fool? When Oscar thought it through he found that it did not matter because what she had done was kind, so Oscar had tried to lift his mother's mourning spirit.

"Do not be sad, my Swan," he said now. "Things are not so bad as they seem. You have given us new hours to enjoy together, and there is no present like the time. We have each other and this day, as silver-white as a pearl, and my hair gone as silver-white as the day. How long will you stay?"

"I must return to Vienna very soon. I have…commitments there, but I won't return until we have decided what to do next, until you are satisfied with the plans for your future."

"Then your commitments will wait a very long time, for only the impossibilities of life can satisfy me now."

He pointed a little farther up the beach. "Let us make our way along the sand. There is a nice little café that the English don't care to frequent at this time of day. They are all in the garden of their hotels having their thick black tea and thin white cake. I often sit alone under the umbrellas and have an Italian tea: Prosecco, so wonderfully like champagne, yet it carries no hangover. Accompanied by crisp, light bread served with tiny, wrinkled olives and tomatoes in oil, it is most refreshing. There I watch the light change across the waters."

When they arrived, having walked in silence along the water's edge, Eleanora found the café pleasant and airy. She positioned her chair slightly behind Oscar's so she could watch him watching the water. Her heart sang to be near him again. And she took comfort that he had seemed so pleased at seeing her. Perhaps Dr. Freud was a pessimist. Perhaps it was all right to hope, just a little, for the impossible. Oscar seemed to require it. Perhaps she did as well.

"I was talking with a man in Vienna," she said. "An interesting man, an Austrian doctor. He says there are three realities we all must face in order to live a psychologically healthy life."

Oscar raised a defensive hand. "I don't want to know them. Health can only be tolerated by the strong."

"Now hear me out, Oscar. He said that first we must give up any notion of immortality."

"Well we have proven him quite wrong on that point already, haven't we Eleanora?"

"Oh Oscar. Do be serious."

"I am never serious after partaking of a meal, and as I take an early breakfast, a reasonably scheduled luncheon, tea, supper, and dinner, I find there is never an occasion to be serious at all. But do go on, my dear.

You were talking about this interesting Austrian and his words to the unwise. What is the second truth that must be faced?"

"He says we are not omnipotent."

"He proves his own point. This route to health is really quite painless. And the third reality?"

"He says we must reconcile ourselves to being of only one gender."

"I hope you shot the villain on the spot."

"Why no. I paid him a rather substantial amount of money for his time and attention."

"Eleanora, I fear the strain of our adventure has addled your wits. You need a long sea voyage or, even better, a night of folly to set you right again. Whoever is this man? That is truly the worst advice I have ever heard."

"His name is Dr. Sigmund Freud and he has discovered a new science. He calls it psychoanalysis and he believes that all our present difficulties have their roots in the traumas of our childhood. He bases his work on the discovery that we have two minds, the conscious and the unconscious."

"I'm afraid you have fallen into the hands of a charlatan, my dear. I could have told you all that without any charge. I was influenced positively beyond repair by reading Balzac when a child, and I've been of two minds about almost everything in my life."

"Nevertheless, I believe him to be a great genius and I have brought you his book; here it is." She pulled from her bag a slim volume, nicely bound, and offered it to Oscar. "It's in German, I'm afraid."

"This becomes worse by the minute." He took hold of her chin, turning her face right and left so as to peruse her features closely. "Yes," he said in mock seriousness, "I see the effects upon your face already. You must be careful to avoid these German books or you will become quite plain." He smiled then. The smile softened her heart.

Oscar took the volume, leafing through it quickly. She saw the glitter of interest in his eyes as they fell randomly onto a page. He snapped shut the book, looking again at the cover. *The Interpretation of Dreams.* Well, what can I say, but thank you, my dear Eleanora. It will be a delicious change from the Marquis de Sade."

"Why do you read such books? And if you do, why speak of them? Do you wish to shock me?"

"No. To shock myself, though nothing does anymore. It's a great pity. Seriously, Eleanora, you must never judge a man by the books he discovers. Only by what he makes of them."

"I take your point."

"Now here is a fresh idea, my Swan. I have heard tell of a Signora Ferriana who resides at certain times in Venice, in some suitably humble abode in the sestiere of Santa Croce. She is a genius at the reading of palms."

Eleanora heaved a great sigh.

"You may sigh for my palmist as I weep for your interpreter of dreams, but we mean to solve the same dilemma: what to do with me. Now I believe Signora Ferriana may have some answers. I would already have sought her out but for a minor inconvenience. I have not enough gold to properly cross her palm in order for her to read mine—many lire, I believe—although I am sure that is less than your Viennese doctor, and to better purpose, for she concerns herself with the telling of future events, not the re-telling of things past."

"But palmistry is mere superstition, Oscar. She can say anything she likes and it has no relevance to reality. Haven't you learned your lesson from that London fortune teller, what was her name?"

"The Sibyl of Mortimer Street. Mrs. Robinson."

"She told you before your jury trials that you would win your case, and I believe you conducted yourself accordingly…all that *bravado!* And look at the results."

"Mrs. Robinson did not say I would win, as you so bluntly put it. Nor did she have the audacity to say that I would be found innocent. She was not such a fool as my dear, departed mother, God rest her soul. She simply predicted that things would turn out for the best in the future. She may yet be proved correct. The century is young."

"You are a hopeless optimist, Oscar."

"Only a hapless pessimist could create such a phrase! Now do come with me, my dear Lady Eleanora, to visit the gifted Signora Ferriana and let us know what is to be. Perhaps she will tell us that we will be lucky in love." Prudence kicked him under the table, but the ploy was a success.

"As you wish, Oscar, as you wish. We will make our way to the Italian edition of your Mrs. Robinson, but on one condition."

"I never agree to conditions. I find them far too stimulating."

"Nevertheless, you must read *The Interpretation of Dreams* while I am in Venice and then tell me what you think of it."

"But people are always so offended when dead men opine about current events."

"I insist, Oscar," she declared, as she handed him money for the palmist.

"And a lovely way you have about it, too."

CHAPTER 10

Oscar and Eleanora made their way by gondola into a true backwater of Venice replete with half-starved cats and half-naked children playing beneath sagging clotheslines. The laundry was strung from house to house across the alleyways that caught no breeze, but instead held a deeply repugnant odor. Eleanora kept a handkerchief to her nose, and Oscar breathed through the cloth of his sleeve as they made their way along the slimy *fondamenta,* deeper into the labyrinth.

"This is a most unseemly place, Oscar," Eleanora protested.

"Indeed we must be particularly cautious," agreed Oscar. "All the best people are to be found here."

"I hardly think so," objected Eleanora, who was not amused.

"Why, *we* are here, are we not? Does that not prove my point?"

"Our folly is undeniable, but no one who is anyone has ever preceded us here, or will ever come behind. I'm certain of it."

"You are wrong, Eleanora. People in search of authenticity come to such places every night. Certainly any woman who resides here must be absolutely authentic."

"Well, something is," replied Eleanora, pressing her handkerchief tighter to her nose.

They arrived at the designated address, a house that appeared ready to pitch itself over onto the cobblestones at the behest of the next strong gale. Oscar rapped with his knuckles on a set of thick wooden doors.

They were soon admitted to a rank hallway by a dark and dirty child of six or seven years, whose gender could not be determined by either its clothing or hair. Oscar shuddered.

"There are always children about when a Gypsy works," he explained. "They are learning the art. But they remind me of the prison children— poor, dirty, unschooled. Please give the child a coin, dear Eleanora."

Eleanora did as Oscar bid her and the urchin pocketed the money without comment. They followed the child up a damp flight of stairs to a murky parlor hung with scarves and carpets. The air, such as it was, was thick with incense.

Signora Ferriana, a Gypsy woman by manner and appearance, was seated before a low fire. She was filing her blood red nails to ever-sharper points. She said something in Romany and the child tossed her the coin. The boy, if it was a boy, then found a corner near the hearth to watch the proceedings, doubtless an apprentice to her art.

Oscar spoke in fluent Italian. "I am a man without a name or a country. You are Signora Ferriana, and I have come to you in order to hear tell of my future, such as it is."

"Be seated, Signore Mysterioso," she indicated, "here across from me on that chair where you can rest your hand on the table. And the lady?"

"She is my protector."

"You need no protection from me." She took his hand without formality, and glanced at it in a perfunctory way. "Only from yourself." She dropped the hand without interest. Eleanora knew men who were repulsed by Oscar's large fleshy hands, with their gentle, almost limp grasp. She knew of women who were frightened by them. Eleanora loved them. She thought of them gently touching her own body, in secret places, and her spirit quickened. The Gypsy shot her an uncanny, knowing glance. Eleanora blushed.

"The money?" queried the Gypsy. Eleanora proffered an envelope with the required sum inside. The woman counted it quickly and the money disappeared into the folds of her garments. The empty envelope fell unheeded to the threadbare carpet. The child edged forward and slid the envelope over to itself with a dirty toe. It explored the envelope in the hope of an overlooked bill, then disappointed, tossed it onto the fire where it sent up a sudden flare of flame. The Gypsy, meanwhile, had closed her eyes and begun to sway back and forth, humming an ancient melody.

Oscar and Eleanora exchanged glances, and she was surprised to see that Oscar showed signs of nervousness. He looks so very handsome now, she thought, as she often did, knowing it was her love for him that enhanced whatever aspect he presented, grooming him and gilding him in her mind's eye to absolute perfection.

The Gypsy ceased her chant. Emerging, glassily changed, amidst a self-induced trance, Signora Ferriana again took hold of Oscar's hand.

"You are a big man," she said, "but your hand is too large even for you. You wanted much and you took much from life—all for your own pleasure."

Oscar looked as if he might speak, but the Gypsy jerked up her free hand, fingers splayed, warding off interruption. "Ssss...do not reply. Do not explain. Do not speak. It is important." Oscar was quelled.

She began examining each of his fingers in turn. "You are a man used to speaking your mind. This is a pleasure for you, but only half the time does it serve your interests. Speak half as much as you do and your life will double in its satisfactions."

Eleanora was watching closely and she saw Oscar grow pale. He seemed as entranced with the Gypsy woman as the woman was with herself. It was then that she recognized the woman's resemblance to Oscar's own mother, Speranza the poetess, the late, wild, Lady Wilde. She had the same dark unkempt hair and pointed features. Did all these sibyls look in some way like her? Was that the spell they cast over him? Eleanora herself could not be more unlike. She took inventory: I am elegant, she thought, not eccentric. I am distinguished, not disreputable. I am thoughtful, not impulsive. I don't write poetry, I prompt it in others. I am yet young and very rich and very smart. I am all the wrong things.

Now the seer peered closely at the lines on Oscar's palm. "Ah!" she exclaimed and visibly jumped away, dropping the hand as if it had burned her own. For a moment her spell seemed to have been broken, but she quickly recomposed herself and then gently lifted Oscar's hand as if it were a wounded animal. "You want to hear what this says? Don't speak! Nod your head. I do not recommend this reading, but you may choose."

Prudence was loud in Oscar's ear. She said to leave. Oscar willfully ignored her.

"Yes," said Oscar, nodding.

"All right. We will continue," declared the sibyl, "but if you will not take my advice for the next ten minutes it is unlikely you will take it for the next ten years. Yes, I see ten years, Signore Mysterioso, maybe a few more, though you will not live to be an old man, your time is borrowed. You see? Your lifeline ends here, in time already past. The rest is silence." She paused. "Until this. This cross of two short lines apart from all the rest, here—is where you will actually die. Fear death by water."

An apt warning, thought Eleanora wryly, given their present locale.

"If I go back into the past, here, I see an early loss, a sister, I think, a change of country, many years of the life you Englishmen call the charmed life, with much success. Then here," she stabbed at a point on his palm, "there is a fateful meeting with a young person, a man, I think; he has led you astray in a terrible way for the line branches to your current fate; you have taken the wrong direction and it has led you to this place."

Oscar nodded again.

She knows who he is! thought Eleanora. She took a deep breath. Who could have gotten so much information to this woman? Who could have supplied her with such personal details? No one knew of their plans to visit this harridan. Except Oscar, of course. Perhaps this was a trick he had arranged to amuse her? But Oscar was shaking and Oscar was not an actor. He was as astonished, more astonished than she was. The woman's performance was uncanny.

"You used to write," declared the Gypsy. "This was a fine thing. You cannot write now. You believe you have lost your genius but this is not so."

The reading continued: "Because you have not been able to write you have felt no reason to continue living; your will to self-destruction arises within you. For yourself, you feel you are done with life, but I have some experience in these matters and I tell you that you will live, but—heed me—you must live another way. Go back to this place, here, where the line branches and go the other way. Fate has given you this opportunity. There may be another romance along this way. I cannot see. A man? If so, you must revile him. A dark lady? Perhaps the one who has accompanied you here? I cannot make it out. You have been a kind man, even a generous one, but now you must devote yourself entirely to the interests of other people, not to your own pleasures. Otherwise there is nothing for you but despair and more despair. Now you may ask me one question if you wish. I do not recommend it."

Prudence, ignored, was silent. Oscar asked his question: "Will I be able to help my sons?"

The seer paused before speaking, giving weight to the words that followed. "Only by your absence."

Oscar gave out a piercing cry and fell sideways from his chair onto the floor. Eleanor came quickly to his side, terrified that he had repeated the damage to his ear first sustained in a similar fall several years previous in the chapel of Reading Gaol. Signora Ferriana ignored them, and began the slow rocking movement and humming sound that had preceded the reading.

"Water, you witch," cried out Eleanora angrily. "Look what you have wrought! Bring us water at once." But the Gypsy appeared not to hear her, continuing to sway and croon. The child brought a ladle of water from a bucket near the fire.

Oscar was beginning to recover consciousness and he pushed the tepid liquid away from his lips. "Prussic acid would be safer," he whispered.

"Do you think you can stand up?" asked Eleanora. He nodded weakly. "Let us leave this ghastly place," she urged.

"A moment, my dear, a moment." Slowly, with Eleanora's able assistance, Oscar pulled himself upright. Though pale and visibly shaken, he seemed otherwise unhurt. The sibyl still moaned.

Suddenly, in his most commanding voice, Oscar turned upon the Gypsy. "Signora Ferriana!" The woman's eyes snapped open. He had her full consciousness and attention.

"Now I will speak," he declared, "and you will listen. Thrice in my life

I have heeded the advice of women: my wife said that if we loved each other we must marry and thus she brought ruin on herself. My mother, when I was the center of scandal, said that I must remain in her sight though everyone else counseled me to flee, and thus she brought ruin on us both. And a Mrs. Robinson, one of your kind, foretold that my prospects were bright when they were black as pitch, and in so doing wrought incalculable harm to me and to many others. Don't speak!"

He raised his palm and the Gypsy once again stared at its center as he continued.

"Your words ring of truth to me. I will heed them. But beware. I will return to you, Signora Ferriana, with the results of your advice. I will lay the consequences on the table where, but a short time ago, I laid my hand. And on that day I will have a reckoning with advice-giving women! Remember me."

Oscar turned and together he and Eleanora hurriedly made their way down the stone steps to the *fondamenta*.

"You won't come back here, Oscar!" pleaded Eleanora as soon as they were clear of the building. "Promise me you will never come here again."

"She said I must live for others, Eleanora, but accept my assurance that it is better for you, and for all who know me, if I remain a man of my word. I will return here with what is now my future—and will then be my past—and I will present it to her, and to the world—in the palm of my hand."

CHAPTER 11

The Case of Lady A
(unpublished)
by Herr Doktor Sigmund Freud

Vienna,
June 1901

I take this opportunity, the first extended break in our schedule of daily treatment, to give shape to my notes on Lady A in preparation for what I hope will be a most interesting case history, and a valuable study of my new, psychoanalytic, method.

Lady A, an unmarried woman of nearly forty, arrived in my consulting room in a state of considerable agitation, poorly masked by the practice of good English manners. She was dressed in the elegant, restrictive fashion of the moment and showed all the signs of considerable wealth and fine breeding. She began our conversation with the pretense of requiring help for "a friend," although it soon became apparent that she was suffering from an elaborate delusional system centering on a deceased friend, the late and notorious writer, Oscar Wilde, whom she referred to as Dear Oscar. She believes that Wilde has survived his own death and is living in Venice under the care of priests to whom she sends considerable financial support.

She was at first resistant to the idea of psychoanalytic treatment, insisting that I should cure the object of her delusion of his homosexuality instead—for she believes herself to be deeply in love with him.

This passion, conceived during Wilde's lifetime, with its inevitable rejections, sexual frustrations, and the dual shocks of his downfall and death are the evident precursors to her nervous breakdown and subsequent delusions.

Our first meeting was inconclusive as to further treatment. However, she soon sent me a note requesting a further consultation. This time she stated that she had formed an intellectual interest in my ideas and desired to come for regular appointments. She reluctantly admitted that she was troubled by periodic melancholia, which she felt psychoanalysis might be able to alleviate. She agreed to a fixed morning hour and has now come daily for six weeks.

Although initially appalled at the idea of discussing her childhood—the educated English classes consider their childhoods of no account—Lady A has revealed the following family history with its obvious bearings upon the present disturbance:

Lady A is the second child and only daughter of Lord and Lady A of H—, an aristocratic tributary of the English royal mainstream. Her elder brother, Bertram, died at the age of ten following his first fox hunt when he mishandled his gun. The gun fired hitting him in the chest and killed him instantly. When Lady A spoke of this deeply traumatic event she did so without discernible emotion. (Note: Lady A interjected at this point that Oscar Wilde had once described the sight of English country gentlemen on a fox hunt as the unthinkable in full pursuit of the uneatable. This jest is an excellent illustration of my theory that all humor has its basis in hostility.)

Following the death of her brother, Lady A's mother became acutely depressed and died soon thereafter, most likely a suicide.

Lady A was eight years old. Her father, forgivably distraught, thought it unsuitable for young Lady A to be brought up by servants and sent her to live with his maiden sister, Lady R, whom my patient refers to as Auntie Gruesome, a "play" on the elderly spinster's given name, Gruzella. This aunt, though very ugly in aspect, treated her kindly, saw to her education, brought her out, and lost interest in her when at the last instant, she refused to marry a young Earl. (Note: this gives evidence of a sexual hysteria already in place.)

Her father settled a large sum of money on Lady A at about the same time and then promptly died.

After about two weeks of regular psychoanalytic sessions, Lady A reported a recurrent dream, which dates from shortly after the death of her brother, Bertram. In the dream, Bertie appears to her, holding the gun that killed him. He stands before her like "a little ghost" and announces that she, Lady A, must now live his life instead of her own. In the dream, she always protests that she doesn't have the right body to live a boy's life, or a man's life, but her brother just laughs and holds up a dead animal—sometimes a fox, sometimes a robin, sometimes a rooster. Bertram then drops the animal, reloads his gun and aims it directly at her. At this point she wakes up in terror. (Note: The dream indicates that Lady A's emotional development is arrested at the age of eight.)

The last occurrence of this dream was about one year ago, the night before the idea to "save Oscar Wilde from his impending death" came over her. The animal held up by Bertram in her dream that night was a phoenix. She refuses to associate to this dream or any other. And her sessions include long periods of silence.

The delusional system that has resulted from her fantasy of the resurrection of Oscar Wilde continues to elaborate. Her most recent resistance to her sessions has taken the form of a journey to Venice in order to implore her imaginary friend, Oscar, to live quietly in his new surroundings and to resume his writing. This journey, real or not, has caused her to miss over a week of the analytic work. When I informed her she would be financially responsible for the missed sessions she did not protest, instead she spoke of Oscar who, she expects, will relieve her of a large sum of money as well, as is his fashion.

The transference implications are obvious.

CHAPTER 12

The Memoirs of Aveline Tartine

So this slip of the Freud amuses you? *Oui?* Once Freud was in fashion even here in Paris; but if I knew him he is the one fashion I will not admit to following. He was a most scandalous sort of Germanic person. How then did I come by this account, you wonder? It was sent to me anonymously from England shortly after Freud's death, one of a number of papers and letters that have come mysteriously into my possession over the years.

Until this week, I did not know who was sending me these papers. They were merely curiosities that arrived at unexpected times and places. Slowly they filled out the story of my Dear Uncle Oscar's last years, for although I knew much at the time when the events were occurring, I did not know all. And when Oscar disappeared in 1912, I never knew what happened to him. But here I sit, in my beautiful boudoir, nearby a box of excellent chocolates begging to be sacrificed to my pleasure, a glass of perfect champagne at my fingertips, and in possession of the knowledge at last.

If you are fortunate enough to have a mystery in your life, then I recommend that you live a very long time.

CHAPTER 13

They were gathered at midnight in Oscar's rooms. Oscar had insisted on midnight and candlelight for the serious discussion that was to ensue. Earlier they had dined on a risotto flavored of lagoon fish and a salad of tender greens, the conversation as light as the bubbling wine.

Timothy Tyharde settled back into an overstuffed chair near the front windows. In daylight, with the curtains pulled back and the shutters thrown open, these windows afforded a magnificent view of the Grand Canal. Oscar pretended never to look out the windows. He said it was not the proper occupation for a gentleman. Timothy was watching Oscar with pleasure. His friend had quickly become lord of his domain, and acting as such, lit a cigarette, and smiled at his guests.

He is still under the spell of his mother, mused Timothy. Lady Wilde had preferred the flattering soft light of candles for her salons. Timothy, who had met her on several occasions, had immediately recognized that she was appallingly vain and histrionic to the point of madness. When a man's own mother doesn't recognize the borders of reality, thought Timothy, it will be difficult for the man, when crisis comes, to know what to do; and crisis was the only time when anyone needed to know the truth of things. The rest of the time one could toddle around in whatever mixture of fantasy and reality one preferred for others neither knew nor cared what anyone else was doing.

His own dear mother, Verity Tyharde, the vicar's wife, had indeed been perfect. Mrs. Tyharde was wont to pronounce that "all men lived in the lap of God." Timothy sighed. He missed his mother, who had died some time ago, without ever having had the satisfaction of seeing her elder son married, but without suffering the repugnance of knowing the reason why.

Timothy returned his mind to the present circumstances, listening to the soft lapping of canal water, just audible, against the outer walls of the palazzo. He was glad he had chosen these particular rooms for Oscar. Affluence expressed in furniture—durable, solid, useful—was reassuring to Timothy.

They were an unlikely group, he mused: an Italian Abbot accompanied by his most humble novice, both men sensually suppressed, one assumed, in the service of God; an aristocratic English lady, doubtless a virgin, who put her purse where her passion lay for she could not put her body there; himself, the son of a Scottish vicar, attracted only to men, celibate by choice; and Oscar, the indefinable Irishman who was at present as sexually subdued as the rest, but, Timothy anticipated, not for long.

They each dutifully held a glass of yellow wine and waited for Oscar to break the silence. Oscar looked superb in this light, as Oscar knew. He leaned against the mantelpiece, in a pose of poise. It was like the penultimate scene in a melodramatic mystery play, with the *dramatis personae* assembled for the resolution of the plot. Life had no plot, Timothy knew, only ceaseless, mindless change with everything falling to bits in the process.

Oscar spoke: "I have made up my mind, on the advice of my friends here congregated, and with the confirmation of the Italian sibyl, to remain living anonymously in Venice," he announced.

Timothy relaxed. Abate Antonio and the novice gave no sign as to what they felt. Eleanora issued a small sigh of relief and smiled in approval. Timothy thought that she looked beautiful with that particular smile. Judging from Oscar's returning eyes, he too was beguiled, for Oscar had always appreciated feminine beauty although, in later life, as a thing apart from Eros. Timothy noticed Eleanora noticing Oscar noticing her. He was enjoying the pantomime.

"However," continued Oscar, "I will in time grow restless here in Venice—a gentleman needs at least three addresses to ensure his contentment. When tedium threatens I must be allowed to travel. I have a plan to see my sons unawares in Germany, or wherever they may be, and I wish to visit my friends, Auguste Rodin in Paris and you, Lady Eleanora, when you are in Vienna. I also need to consult with a physician there, a Dr. Sigmund Freud."

Eleanora gasped in surprise, and Timothy raised an eyebrow, but neither chose to interrupt Oscar as he spun out his unlikely future.

"No one will notice me as I go about. I am quite certain of that. My aspect is quite changed, and suited up in ordinary ill cut clothing and traveling penuriously, I will pass as an average man. I once remarked that to pass through life unnoticed is the most ostentatious form of obscurity, and I tend, as you all know, toward the ostentatious. I don't know how to pay for these journeys except through your continued consideration, nor how to repay you for the monies you have already invested in my resurrection, nor how to pay off the debts that follow me beyond my supposed grave, but I shall do so. Perhaps one day I shall be able to sit down again, pen in hand, and lie at length. Or perhaps if I cannot write I can turn my hand to some other suitably dishonest means of livelihood. Can we all agree to this?"

"I have heard tell of this man, Freud," objected the Abate. "He is a Jew, and worse, an atheist. Though you are but a reluctant son of the true faith I must, as your spiritual advisor, protest any proposed dealings with this man. His theories are anathema."

"Lady Ashburton has met him," responded Oscar. "She seems quite taken with him. Eleanora, is he an anti-Christ?"

"Sigmund Freud is controversial," she replied coolly, then sipped her wine, as if to prevent herself from saying anything more. Abate Antonio continued his argument as if she had not spoken. "He believes that children engage in—I cannot bring myself to say it." The novice squirmed uncomfortably at his side, sensing the import.

"Sex," supplied Oscar. "And he doesn't quite say they engage in sex, only that they have sexual longings, sexual dreams. In my experience, that is quite true."

"I do not agree, nor do I think it seemly for a man in your position, or for any Christian man, to say such a thing. But you are a willful person,

Mr. Wilde, and if you wish to seek out this charlatan I cannot prevent you from doing so any more than I can stop you from consorting with fortunetellers. I can only warn you against such sinister company for the good of your immortal soul."

"Thank you, Abate," replied Oscar sincerely, "but as Christ did not heed such warnings in his day and ran about with all the worst sort of scoundrels, I am afraid I will follow in his footsteps."

Oscar is re-finding his fettle, thought Timothy, quite happily, as he watched the Abate silenced in the face of the astonishing comparison.

"I didn't know you had read Dr. Freud's book, Oscar," said Eleanora. "Will you really go to see him? With pardon, Abate, but Dr. Freud has discovered some truths about the workings of the mind; I am sure of it. I think he may prove helpful to Oscar."

Timothy, who had also heard tales of the infamous Dr. Freud, thought it would be a fine example of the blind leading the blind, in this case, straight into the Vienna woods. Timothy now began to perceive the outlines of Eleanora's secret. She had been going to see Sigmund Freud herself. Leave it to Eleanora, he mused, to ferret out, and then attach herself to, the most provocative man in any city in which she resides.

"Well, I cannot agree with you, Lady Ashburton," responded Abate Antonio, recovering from his astonishment, "nor am I entirely in agreement with this whole plan for Oscar. Why, if you will be so kind to explain to me, is anonymity so essential? Surely you and Mr. Tyharde broke no laws in saving a man's life."

"Oscar's creditors and those who buried him may think differently, Abate," countered Eleanora.

"They are in France and England. We are in Italy."

"How delightful to have a spiritual advisor with both a pragmatic turn of mind, and a knowledge of geography," interjected Oscar.

"And as Mr. Wilde plans to settle his debts," continued the Abate, "I cannot see the harm in his leading a truthful life instead of climbing about on this web of deception which you all seem to insist upon. Go humbly and truthfully in the world and all will be forgiven."

"Begging your pardon, Abate," said Oscar, drawing himself up to his considerable height, "but for my deceptions I have been forgiven many times over; it is the truth of who I am that has been judged and found unforgivable. I have been, since my trials, an embarrassment to all who knew me, a problem to which there is no solution. The world needs a rest from Oscar Wilde. It needs to reconsider its entire relationship to me and to what I have come to represent. So, out of sight, I shall be kept in mind. That is how it should be and I see no harm in it. I am quite certain that there exists no commandment against anonymity. And what could be more humble, now that I think of it, than not to possess even one's own identity?"

"There is truth to what you say, Mr. Wilde. We brothers give up our worldly identity when we enter the monastery, but you plan to move about in the world."

"As a ghost. And not even as my own ghost." Timothy saw Oscar's eyes light up. "Why, yes, that's it!" exclaimed Oscar. "I have an idea. It's a very small idea, but like all small ideas it has enormous consequences, and what a relief it is to have an idea at all! I thought I should never have another one as long as I re-lived." He savored a taste of his wine, and then leaned forward conspiratorially, "I shall call myself after a ghost; a ghost that I, myself, created: *The Canterville Ghost*. Yes, and in deference to your monastic ministrations, Abate, I shall call myself Francis. Francis Canterville it shall be. Names mean a great deal to a writer. What do you think? Perhaps we should have a christening?"

Smiling at the echo from *The Importance of Being Earnest*, the Abate replied "I think the idea of adult christenings works better in fiction than in reality."

"Everything does," declared Oscar, "that is what fiction is for."

"I am glad to hear you speak of yourself as a writer, Oscar, I mean Francis," said Timothy, speaking for the first time. He liked the name that Oscar had chosen for himself, and for a moment wished he could rename himself, live elsewhere, begin his own life anew. How strange, he thought, to arrive at an hour when I find myself in envy of Oscar Wilde.

"Oh yes, I am sure I will be able to write again as Francis Canterville. It's a divine name. It has a music of its own. Oh, isn't life wonderful, especially when one has died? I always loved life, even when it didn't love me, and now that I am dead I can truly savor it. Can we all agree then?"

"There is one other matter." It was Eleanora speaking.

"What is it, Eleanora? You sound troubled," asked Oscar.

Here it comes, thought Timothy.

"It's about Lord Alfred Douglas," she said.

"Bosie," whispered Oscar, turning as pale as his own fictitious ghost.

"You must remain dead to him, too."

Stillness had dropped into the room at the mention of Bosie. A stillness that seemed to silence even the waters outside the palazzo. Everyone had stopped breathing.

Oscar looked into his wine. It was he who drew the first breath, which he let out slowly before looking up.

"I believe there are two kinds of people in the world," he said. "I suppose the two sets are of equal value when everything is taken into account, but I can only understand the kind that I am, and that is a creature of passion. I know of the others, those who love and work and carry on the world's business in the normal sort of way. They often love deeply, they usually work hard; some are good, some bad, but they all assume they are the only kind of people. We of the second variety know, have always known, that we are different. We are not out of control, or weak, or dishonorable by nature, though we often appear that way. We have the gift and the curse of passions. When passion takes hold of us it takes over our minds, our hearts, our bodies and our wills, all for its own purposes. Sometimes the passion is divine. You know about that, Brother Paul." His head swung to face the startled novice. "You have the divine fire within you. You love God with all your heart and all your soul and you would die for him, would you not?"

He did not wait for a reply. "You, on the other hand, Abate, love God well and honorably. You might even choose to die for him, but there is the difference. You could choose. You have choice. Not the little brother here. He has no will at all in the force of his passion. I know this from watching you both for many months."

He turned to face Timothy. "Timothy, here, is like the Abate, a good and steady man with a great heart and a kind soul, but the fire of passion has never burned within him." This, thought Timothy sadly, was true.

Oscar's eyes met Eleanora's. "You, Lady Ashburton, are like me. You are helpless when you are gripped by passion. Is that not so?" Timothy knew that Oscar knew that he controlled Eleanora utterly, and Timothy blushed for her. Could the Abate see this, the novice? Eleanora returned Oscar's gaze unflinchingly.

"You would do anything for the man you love, Eleanora. You would die for him," Oscar continued. "It does not matter how badly he treats you, who else he loves, what others say, you would deny him nothing." Eleanora lowered her eyes at last, as if to acknowledge the truth of what he said.

Oscar walked to the end of the room where Timothy was sitting. He pulled open the draperies and pushed open the shutters. Fresh air, sparkling reflections, water music surrounded him as he turned to face the group. "I am like Eleanora. I am like good, young Brother Paul. I have no will when it comes to that which I love. Once, Lord Alfred Douglas, my own dear boy, Bosie, possessed me, and I was utterly his. I miss that so."

Timothy saw a solitary teardrop make its way down Eleanora's cheek. She did not pay heed to it, but looked back at Oscar as though to say, *Even this I can hear from your lips, even this, and not flinch.*

"But as long as Bosie does not know I live, I will try with what strength I have to stay apart from him. I have tried before, many times, and I have always failed. I know that Bosie would not be able to keep our secret. He would sell the story to the newspapers for what he could get and gamble the money away. He would then ask me to die and come to life yet again if he saw more profit in it. This I know like I know my new name. I can, of course, hope that something in my heart has changed. When last Bosie and I were together there were only embers of passion; perhaps now, only a spark remains and will soon fly up and die. I do not know and cannot trust my heart. Perhaps the doctor in Vienna could cure me of this attraction, but at what price, I ask you, at what price? For Bosie was my muse, my inspiration, my poetry, my life!"

Oscar was at his best, observed Timothy. He had made them all miss Bosie!

"However, Decency in the disguise of a Gypsy woman, declares that

I must go another way at the crossroads; she says that I must live only for others. She has frightened me with her clairvoyance. She has threatened me into selflessness and terrified me into altruism. Usually that task is left to the church, begging your pardon, Abate. And so for you, my friends, I promise to try to hide myself from the object of my life's passion. But I ask you, dear Lady Eleanora, could you do it?"

"No," she replied solemnly, "not as yet. I live for his smile."

"I am so sorry," he said softly.

They beheld each other for a long minute in perfect understanding, and in perfect pain.

Timothy, who could stand the melodrama no longer, stood up. "Well we are agreed then: anonymity, Francis Canterville, limited travel, Sigmund Freud, and a return to writing if Oscar re-finds his ability to lie fluently. How about a dessert?" he suggested. "The maid has prepared a tiramisu, I believe."

"Brother Paul and I must return to the island without further ado," said the Abate. "All that can be said has been said. I will pray for you Oscar, now Francis. Send word whenever you are in Venice, and whenever you depart. You always have a refuge with us, whatever our differences of thought may be. But you are well counseled. Would that religion had the power of the gypsy woman over your soul."

"I must go as well," said Eleanora. "The night train departs Mestre at three. I will transfer additional funds to Timothy's account in Venice to meet your expenses, Oscar. Let me know if they become insufficient. Travel soon to Vienna. I will miss you until then." And with those words, she departed, with her usual grace, along with Abate Antonio and the novice.

Oscar turned to Timothy. His face carried a look of deep concern. "Was I cruel, Timothy? I know I was eloquent, but I have no wish to be cruel."

"The situation is cruel."

"Yes. That is so. I wonder why God designed us so. It seems like a game does it not? One where all the players love the wrong people, get horribly hurt, and the spectators smile through their tears until their own number is called. It makes me sad about God. And what about you?

It's plain enough how Eleanora got herself into this plot, but whatever were you thinking? Your reputation would be ruined if it were revealed that you were associated with me at all, let alone under these circumstances. What would become of your mission house then?"

"It was Eleanora's idea to save you. She counted on my missionary's soul…She couldn't stand to lose you, and I liked you both well enough to help. Its been a terrific distraction for me—plotting in Paris, skulking about with bribes, meeting Rodin, traveling thither and yon, letting this palazzo, spending Eleanora's money. The truth is, that since my mother died and my brother soon after, I have been subject to melancholy. My work in the East End is fulfilling, but it's endless and feels, at times, hopeless. There are so many hungry people waiting for their bowl of soup. Oh, I save up enough now and then to buy a fine piece of porcelain or a good chair for myself, but they give only momentary pleasure, situated as they are in my third rate flat. This adventure has left me scant time to be unhappy, and as to my reputation, well, without a mother to worry about it, a reputation doesn't seem to matter very much."

"You are right. The death of one's mother is a great liberation. At long last one feels allowed to take great risks, even to die. I do wish I had waited until my mother was safely in heaven before I went straight to hell. But let us find a way to lighten your dark mood."

Oscar put his arm gently around Timothy's shoulders and for the first time Timothy felt a faint trace of the feeling he knew other men had felt for Oscar, and that he sometimes felt for other men. The feeling frightened him. It was a complication in their relationship that neither of them could afford.

"Come outside, Tim," encouraged Oscar, "where there is darkness, there is Hope. It is a moonless night and we will glide across the lagoon's marmoreal waters past pillars of undulating stone. We will ride in a gondola of ebony, recalling the golden days of our youth, and of our happiness. Your melancholy will fly with the dawn, for nowhere in the world is dawn more beautiful than here in Venice, and Beauty cures Melancholy."

CHAPTER 14

Francis Canterville in his Italian workingman's clothing was even less recognizable than he had been as Sebastian Melmoth in his monk's habit. He kept himself from the *fondamente* and *campi* during normal working hours, so as not to draw attention to his idleness. He spent the days rereading all of Balzac, Dante, Shakespeare, Huysmans, all his favorite authors, sent to him by Timothy and Eleanora.

On a whim, as the summer arrived, he had begun to poke about in the neglected back garden. Four years ago, when he had been released from Reading Gaol, both the laburnum and lilac were flowering and he had rejoiced to be free among their scented glory for the single day he had remained in England. Now he cultivated an appreciation for more exotic blooms, enjoying the papery redness of frangipani and the tiny fragrant blossoms of the miniature fruit trees. He remembered that once as a guest at a fashionable country house party he had sat up all night with a wilting anemone so that it would not die alone. Well, so he had said at breakfast. He had certainly *meant* to. He smiled at the memory of his frivolous days, and mused that he who had always loved flowers had never gardened. Gardening was work. And work was ungentlemanly.

Now he learned to encourage the gardenia bushes so that they soon flowered to his touch. Each milky blossom became a friend to him, and he mourned the first touch of brown on a petal's edge. Brother Paul, who came regularly from the Isola to bring him his mail, observed him in the garden and, when next he came, brought bulbs and roots. Oscar dutifully planted narcissus and lilies for a spring he hoped he would not share with them, for even as he dug into the earth he was preparing himself to wander.

To this end, in the earliest hours of morning when no one but fishermen were about, he often took himself off alone in a rowing boat to explore the uninhabited islands of the lagoon where he made friends of lizards and seabirds. If his travels took him nearby, he would lunch with the Abate at the monastery or take tea with Fra Ricardo and Hector, the parrot, in happy attendance. Then he would make the long journey back across the water in the hot mists of the afternoon when everyone else was asleep.

Nightly he walked. The journey, around the rim of the city if uninterrupted, took him two and a quarter hours, but he often entered one of the obscure, smoke-filled trattorias along the circuit, the kind of eating establishment that served the local populace. He knew himself to be neither happy nor unhappy as he ate his lonely meals. He was thinking.

Looking back he knew that prison had for a time made him mad. During that time he had written letters wrought of rage, bursting with anger and insult, to all who had loved him, and these from the hand of a man who, in his right mind, never blamed anyone for anything, for he loved life and he loved the human tragedy every bit as much as the human comedy and had been willing to play his part in both.

The long letter to Bosie expressing the worst of his wrath had disappeared, into a fireplace he fancied, for that was Bosie's way with unpleasant realities. When they had been briefly reunited after his release from prison, the letter had not been mentioned. Of course, the letter Bosie had burned was only a typewritten copy. The original document, painfully hand written on thin, blue Reading Gaol stationary, still existed. His friend Robbie Ross had it for safekeeping amongst his other papers. The letter served as his apology, his explanation of the fateful plunge from fame to infamy, and would someday find its place in the archives of Posterity; so Patience assured him.

Robbie Ross, he was told, was busy restoring his literary work into print and rehabilitating his reputation as a poet and playwright. Good old Robbie. Word had it that the Germans were about to produce *Salomé*. In the process, his bills were getting paid. This was just what he needed, he mused, excellent credit under the wrong name!

Oscar knew that he had disappointed Robbie Ross by loving Bosie Douglas more. He knew he had disappointed Bosie by not being able to rally his passion after prison. He knew he had disappointed Eleanora by not recognizing the nature of her love for him, and by not responding to it when he did. He had disappointed Timothy with his inability to write. There were false starts at plays and poems, of course, for ideas still came to him, but his Muse was fled or dead or wed to another. To his family, what was left of it, and to his grieving friends, he had died a monumental disappointment. Perhaps that was the unacknowledged price of public greatness: to disappoint everyone one loves in private.

He glanced around the trattoria at the other diners: all men, all hardy, some handsome in their sea-hardened way. This was certainly not the Savoy Grill, but the food was plentiful, the Prosecco cheap, and the light reflecting from the nearby waters danced upon the ancient walls in a most charming way.

He noticed the men without desire, barely able to remember the times when, excited by their masculinity, he would have searched for the special gleam returned in the eyes of another. After he had come to love men, he could no longer respond to the enticements of women, and now all forms of excitement eluded him. His sexuality had died with his death. Or perhaps the friar had mixed something fastidious into his herbal teas that vanquished carnal desire forever. He felt himself to be like a child, not yet awakened to the pleasures of the flesh. Or like an old, old man. He was burnt out, like a candle that had been halved and then lit from the middle in both directions. No wonder his muse had abandoned him. He had disappointed even his muse. These were the thoughts he mulled along with his wine, and picked apart along with his fish.

And then the startling young man entered the trattoria.

The man, a boy really, was English. Oscar discerned this by the cut of his clothes. And he was rich. Oscar perceived this by the quality of the cloth. And he was in disgrace. Oscar deduced this by the way the lad carried himself. His movements were hesitant and slightly furtive. He was not so young as Bosie had been when first presented to Oscar, nor was he as beautiful. Few young men could successfully compete with Bosie's golden hair and violet eyes. Bosie wore the face Oscar had created three years before they had met, the face of Dorian Gray. Whenever Oscar created something truly original it seemed to manifest a short time later, in reality. He had long known this startling fact about his work, but not what to make of it.

However, this new boy was of his own making and had arrived of his own accord. He had dark hair, made darker by contrast with his pale blue eyes. There was a lost look about him and he was, of course, irresistible.

Thoughts of his own antiquity, his own mortality, his own celibacy, instantly disappeared. Oscar stared, holding onto his fork until he could grip it no longer. Then, he released his grip and fell in love.

He watched and waited like a hood-eyed bird of prey. The young man went to the bar and ordered a drink—whiskey and soda, not popular in Italy, and causing some consternation behind the bar. He then hunched over the amber liquid, looking neither to the right nor to the left.

Oscar noticed his own glass was dry. Ignoring Patience who had begun to keen, he made his way to the end of the bar asking for another glass of Prosecco in his faultless Italian. The youth did not appear to notice him, lost as he was in his own sorrows. Oscar returned to his table and his enjoyment of the young man's profile. At the bar, the drink began to embolden the lad, and he began to venture an occasional glance over his surroundings. Oscar's anticipation grew as he waited for the boy's eyes to enter his own.

Prudence was having a fit, flailing and sputtering in an imprisoned corner of his mind. Against his will, he remembered the advice of the Gypsy: the past predicts the future; when you come again to the same cross in the road—go the other way. Oscar directed his eyes away from the young man and down to the uneven stone floor, determined to stare at the edge of his boots until the object of his reawakened desire had left the trattoria. It was the most difficult thing he had ever willingly done.

"Basta?" It was the barman speaking to the boy, noting the empty glass.

"No. Another. Per favore." The young man's voice was musical. Oscar looked up. The barman poured. The young man lifted his drink, swung around on his barstool, and their eyes met and held over the rim of the tumbler. It was intoxication. The boy slowly lowered his glass and then, as if sleepwalking, made his way to Oscar's table. "May I join you?" he asked shyly.

"It appears you already have."

"I know you."

"Do you?"

The boy's voice dropped to a whisper: "You are Oscar Wilde."

"I know."

"I thought you were dead."

"So did I."

"But how is it you are here? This is the most utterly wonderful happening, the most amazing occurrence!"

"I think that is the kindest thing anyone has ever said to me."

"Is it, why?"

"I thought my tale was ended," replied Oscar. "Why did I not know you in England?"

"I am of the wrong class."

"Beauty is a classless society."

"Perhaps, but I am not from good society, nor am I a servant, so there was no common floor on which we could have met. I fell through the cracks, so to speak."

"But you are educated, wealthy."

"I went to the wrong college and my money comes from the wrong place."

"There is no wrong place for money to come from, only for it to go to, and over that one can quibble. There are, it is true, wrong colleges. Where does your money come from?"

"From trade."

"White slave trade? Opium? Or perhaps is it something evil, like clocks or clerical collars?"

"My father owns several manufacturing companies. Brass fittings for carriages, medical implements, that sort of thing."

"And by your demeanor I can tell that you will not enter into this disgraceful family business, making of yourself, by non-implication, an outcast."

"I write music."

"A most fitting occupation for a gentleman. Families of the merchant classes always bellow in moral indignation whenever a son wishes to become a gentleman."

"And I refuse to marry. That is the real cause of their distress."

"No one who isn't anyone marries these days. Think no more about it. We will be great friends instead. But you must not tell anyone you have seen me."

A knowing look flashed across the young man's face. "Will you promise the same?"

"A deal, as your father is doubtless inclined to say, has been struck. Where were you hiding before you came to stay with me in my beautiful palazzo on the Grand Canal?"

"A small hotel with a large bill on the Rio de San Vio."

Feeling quite like his old self for the first time since London, Oscar handed the young man all of Eleanora's money. "Here. Do your Christian duty and relieve the anxieties of the poor innkeeper. This will not make either of you any the happier. If when you come to me, you find that your kindly impulse persists, I, too, am in need of relief, though of a pagan sort which carries the potential for a large amount of mutual pleasure, and pleasure taken in sufficient quantities has been known to produce happiness."

Unlike Bosie Douglas this young man was full of effusive appreciation. Oscar silenced him with a gentle wave of the hand. He gave the young man his address. "What is your name?"

"Charles. Charles Redfield."

"Charming. Mine is Francis. Francis Canterville."

"Part saint, part ghost."

"You are quick, Charles, quick. I reckon your wrong college did right by you. One last question?"

"Of course."

"How on earth did you recognize me? Particularly as we have never met?"

"It was your walk."

"My walk?"

"When you came over to the bar for another glass of Prosecco, you didn't think I was watching you, but I was. I once saw you walking on The Strand. You were pointed out to me by a friend. It was the day before the opening of *An Ideal Husband*, which I then managed to attend. It was my first play, actually. You were very naughty about musicians in that play."

"That seems likely. What did I say?"

"'Musical people are so absurdly unreasonable. They always want one to be perfectly dumb at the very moment when one is longing to be absolutely deaf.' I told it for weeks afterwards to amuse my friends, well, until…"

"Until my trials began."

"Yes. Well, as I was saying, there you were walking along, the famous Oscar Wilde, and you were carrying a parcel."

"A parcel?"

"A square box about the size of a shoe box. Wrapped up in brown paper and string."

"How shocking! I must have been terribly distracted to have done such an ordinary thing. It shows the recklessness of my nature to have cared so little for my reputation."

"Your walk was distinctive. Unforgettable, really. Perhaps it's my interest in rhythms. All poetic meters arise from ways of walking or dancing. But you know this. I have always wondered what was in the parcel."

"No idea, Charles. I can't picture the thing at all. Perhaps it was a three volume novel, now forever lost."

"Surely nothing is lost forever."

"Ah, the optimism of youth." Oscar sighed. "I had almost forgotten. Go now, dear Charles, and free yourself from all remnants of respectability. Then come, as quick as your mind, to me."

"Thank you, Mr. …uh…Canterville. Thank you, ever so much."

Oscar bowed his head and through lowered lashes watched as Charles Redfield left the trattoria with nary a backward glance. The voices in his head were busy: Prudence, quite shocked by what had just occurred, caused him to wonder if he should ever see the lad again. Patience, far more relaxed by nature, noted that it had been lovely for Oscar to feel his old self again if only for these few minutes.

Oscar smiled, for among their voices he heard another—Eros.

How he had missed him.

Note from Oscar Wilde

VENICE, ITALY
February, 1912

It was a breathtaking experience to be in bed with Charles Redfield. (Yes, Charles, should you ever chance to read my memoir that is what I say.) Charles had a perfect profile. So rare among the middle classes. And he was young, with a sleek, hard body that I engraved upon my memory with kisses. He revitalized me in a way that monks and women and long walks for my health could not do. And to him I remain eternally grateful.

I wondered, of course, if I could find a remnant of love for Charles or if my heart had fabric enough for only one great passion, Lord Alfred Douglas. Alas, Charles and all the others, before and since, were but romances cut from other, lesser cloth.

I was to see Bosie Douglas again, of course. But under remarkable circumstances that would leave my heart, once again, in shreds.

CHAPTER 15

The Memoirs of Aveline Tartine

It was three years after our first meeting that I was to again see Oscar Wilde, whom I had adopted over the cakes as my Dear Uncle Oscar. That would make it 1903. I don't know who was more surprised—for I, in the arms of Auguste Rodin, had grown from the child that Oscar had first known into womanhood, and he had come back from the grave.

He arrived in a coach-and-four that pulled into the courtyard on a beautiful summer morning. The coach stopped only long enough for a large lumbering man of late middle years to descend onto the cobblestones. He wore a beard as white as Carrara marble. It contrasted pleasantly with the deep tan of his complexion. He carried one small leather satchel and his overcoat was of a handsome cut.

I witnessed his arrival from my bedroom window on the third floor. He seemed familiar to me, but I could not immediately place him. I turned from the window and called my maid into attendance.

"Madeleine, who is M. Rodin receiving today? Someone for a portrait bust?"

"It's a mystery to me, Mademoiselle," replied the servant who had become oddly taciturn of late. "The master has mentioned nothing to the staff about a visitor."

"I've seen that man somewhere before."

The maid leaned out of the window beside me and peered at the stranger. "I do not recognize him, Mademoiselle. But he looks like an artist, yes?"

"Yes. The hat is all wrong for any other kind of person. That is an Italian suit. Now who could it be?"

She shook her pretty head in puzzlement.

"Do up my hair so that I am presentable," I commanded. I waited for Madeleine to assure me that I was always more than presentable, but the maid merely went to get her combs. I was not pleased with this.

Ten minutes later, my displeasure dispelled by my own attractiveness, and brimming with curiosity, I descended the staircase. No one but the servants was about the house, and the studio yielded only Rodin's assistants and their charges of marble and bronze. "Where are M. Rodin and his visitor?" I asked repeatedly. No one seemed to know. Annoyed, I went out to search the paths that wound energetically through the thick shrubbery. Surely two grown men could not vanish so completely and so swiftly, I thought, but I found no trace of them in the garden.

Vexed, I called out: "Auguste! Auguste, where are you?" No reply was forthcoming. Foiled, I returned to the conservatory and demanded tea. I sat, tapping my fingers in dismay on the impassive tabletop.

Since becoming the mistress of Auguste Rodin and, thereby, the mistress of La Folie I had enjoyed a growing sense of power. Of course, there was Rose Beuret with her son in Meudon to be endured. Rodin's wife, people called her, though she was not his wife, only his long, bad habit. He had not even recognized their son, also called Auguste, but without an iota of the master's talent. Rodin's most recent mistress had hung herself, but Camille Claudel was not so distant a memory as to be forgotten entirely, not with her image carved and cast all about the place; and there were the other models who came at Auguste's behest and often went at my command if I judged them too willing. I was now foremost in Rodin's thoughts and feelings, and I had become used to knowing exactly where he was.

In the beginning Rodin had been reluctant to initiate a sexual affair with so young a person. He respected my convent upbringing as I did not. He was sensitive to my extreme innocence, which I was desperate to have done with, preferably by hard and fast living. And he was at the

time engaged in other, less harrowing, affairs from which I was determined to liberate him. I had time and beauty on my side, both strong.
He had principles and the lessons of experience on his, both weak. In
due time I prevailed.

When he fell, it was with a crash that would shatter stone. He loved
me now, so he sculpted me now. He drew me, and painted me, and
molded me to his satisfaction. I let him have his way with me in every
light, in every position, in every medium including my own substance
and this was the second greatest pleasure I had ever known. The exercise
of my power over him was the first. He fawned on me. He celebrated me.
He treasured me. I, Aveline Tartine, the hazelnut tart, the stray squirrel,
the foundling child had become, in just three year's passing, a woman
made of marble.

As I reached for a strawberry teacake in the humid conservatory
it suddenly came to me and I knew who had stepped down from the
hansom cab. It was my Dear Uncle Oscar! It could be no other, yet his
death, so soon after our short sweet meeting, had been written of in
every newspaper. My grief, even on so short an acquaintance, had been
deep. Auguste had tried to comfort me. What was it he had said? I had
thought it strange at the time. Now I remembered: he had said, "Have
heart, little squirrel, things are not always quite as they seem." And he
had kissed away my tears of mourning, and taken my virginity, and
kissed away my tears of pain.

Things were, indeed, not what they seemed. Oscar, as heedless of his
obituaries in death as he had once been of his reviews in life, was alive!
And he was hidden away somewhere in this house or on these grounds
with Auguste Rodin. But where? My pulse quickened. Rilke, Auguste's
new secretary, the strange Austrian poet, would know. I sent Madeleine
to find him, with a command to come at once.

Rilke soon arrived, happy to be called for in any way that might serve
Rodin, whom he worshiped as one would worship a God. He stood
before me, full of Teutonic compliance and correctness. I had little use
for him under normal circumstances.

"Monsieur Rodin is entertaining a guest, an artist from Italy, by all
appearances. Where are they?"

"I know nothing of this, Mademoiselle. He mentioned nothing of the kind to me."

"I saw the gentleman arrive. Now where could they have gone?"

"You know, Mademoiselle Tartine, from time to time Rodin disappears. I cannot find him. He reappears as mysteriously as he vanishes. Do you suppose there is a hidden chamber, somewhere in the house?"

"I have thought of this myself," I replied, although I hadn't. It had taken a poet to imagine such a thing. The idea that Auguste kept secrets from me was intolerable. Rilke was right about the disappearances. I had once taken Auguste to task about them, and in the only angry interchange between us he had snapped: "Even a man has private functions, Aveline. Let me alone!"

To Rilke, I said only: "Let us search."

"But where?" asked the poet quite helplessly.

"We must look at the floors."

"The floors? Do you think the chamber is under the floors?"

"No. I think that floors show wear, and if we inspect them closely the wear will lead us where."

"Cleverly put, Mademoiselle Tartine."

"Oh, *do* call me Aveline. You Austrians are always so formal. I dislike formality. It reminds me of the convent."

"As you wish, Mademoiselle. Aveline."

We began to walk about La Folie together looking for clues on the carpets and floorboards.

"But if we find the Master, will he not be displeased with us?" Rilke worried.

"He is never displeased to see me," I declared, hiding any anxiety I held on the matter.

"I cannot say the same for myself," murmured Rilke.

"Here! Look!" I cried indicating a well-worn area on the parquet of the sitting area, to the side of the main dining room. "Look how the scuff marks go right into the mirrors." I leaned an ear against the wall. "They are in there, all right," I informed the troubled secretary. "I can hear laughter." The sound of their laughter had made me very angry. I could not abide the exclusion.

"Where is the latch? The catch?" I demanded impatiently, but Rilke only shrugged and began to back away. I reached up to the only prospect, a loose knot of wood to the side of the mirror, pressed upon it, and to my satisfaction saw the panel swing back to reveal Auguste and Oscar, wreathed in pipe smoke, deep in pleasant conversation, in what appeared to be a fully outfitted gentleman's study.

Oscar looked at me in surprise, and rose as was the custom of the day. "It looks as if our little squirrel has once again found her way past the walls," he said with good humor, and got up to welcome me. Auguste, I noted, was less happy at being discovered. He did not get up. Rilke had scuttled away at the first sign of the swinging panel and was not to be seen. I stepped into the study and the panel closed behind me and I decided to set aside my pique with Auguste in favor of my astonishment and joy at the reunion.

"Dear Uncle Oscar! Why have you been hiding yourself away from me for so long? I thought you were forever gone. I shall never forgive you!"

"You must learn to forgive, little squirrel. Forgiveness is not so difficult. It is simply a matter of giving up all hope of a better past."

I put my arms around the large man, and felt him return my happiness. "Where have you been? Here? In these secret chambers?"

"I have been in ephemeral Venice. I go next to solid Vienna, then return to Venice where a young friend awaits me, or at least I hope he does. Being myself, I could not resist the temptation to visit Paris to see my dear friend Auguste, and my dear adopted niece, Aveline, who has grown into such a spectacular woman in my absence."

He stood back to survey me further—the smart dress, and cascade of dark curls, perfectly arranged as I required.

"What an excellent influence I have been on you," he declared. "I wish all my relations turned out so well."

"We must have a party, a ball. We must celebrate your return to life."

"That will not be possible, Aveline," declared Rodin in a solemn voice. Auguste seldom denied me any whim, and I was taken aback. He continued: "Oscar is now leading a life more suited to a man of international espionage than to a man of international literature. Only his closest friends know that he is alive. And he wishes for this to remain so."

"Oh but why?" I cried. My vision of the glittering party faded away and I felt the disappointment keenly.

It was Oscar who responded to my distress. "Dear little hazelnut, I once wrote that one can survive everything except death, and live down everything except a good reputation. I was wrong on both counts. Here in Paris a scandal can sometimes be forgiven, but not my particular kind of scandal. I have lost the heart to face any more people who, by virtue of thinking of themselves as good, feel a moral obligation to treat me badly."

"But Dear Uncle Oscar—"

"And there are those," he continued, "those I love, who would be hurt more by my return to life than by my supposed death. I desire only to stay here a little while with you in peace, and in obscurity."

I sat down thoughtfully, needing some time to take in his words, to find my place in this new scheme of his life. Oscar sat also and went to work relighting his pipe. I noticed the changes in Oscar: the snow-white hair, the teeth restored to a healthy whiteness, the destruction around the eyes, the sadness that had crept into his mannerisms, his even gentler tone of voice.

"People can be villainous, though I don't understand why they should hate you for loving men. I do know all about that now, you know."

"Aveline, my dear," interjected Rodin, "perhaps this is not a suitable topic of conversation, no?"

"It is just that kind of attitude, Auguste, that begins all the trouble," I countered, my anger at his secret keeping just below the surface, coloring my tone on this unrelated issue. "Why shouldn't we speak of it? What can be wrong with love?"

Rodin turned away and puffed at his pipe. Now he was angry, for I had dared to challenge him in front of his guest. Good, I thought. It serves him right.

Oscar, watching the skirmish, felt it was incumbent upon him to speak: "It was not my loving men that outraged society, Aveline, it was that for years I had poked fun at society, on stage and off, yet I appeared to care for my place within it. This seeming hypocrisy annoyed them. And then I flouted society's golden rule."

"What rule is that?" I queried, eager, like all those of lowly birth, to know the customs of the aristocracy.

"Simply put: do unto others whatever you like, but do it discreetly, and only with members of your own class—parlor maids excepted, if you happen to be a gentleman."

I noted Rodin shift uncomfortably in his chair.

"It was my intrigues with the wrong kind of man that society found intolerable", Oscar continued. "I was as genuinely interested in stable boys as I was in princes, and it was this outrage, not my inclinations per se, that engendered the uproar. I'm through with Society, Aveline. I wish for the quiet pleasures of good friends, good food, good wine—and the doing of good deeds; perhaps through my writing if I can ever get it started again."

"You talk like the driver of a horseless carriage that has stalled on the boulevard and needs a good cranking up."

"A very apt description of my writing at present. Perhaps some time in Paris will be all the crank I need."

"Then it seems we have just the suite of rooms you require," I said at last. Auguste nodded in agreement, but looked grim. I knew we were in for a fight when we were next alone. We would go hammer on marble.

Nevertheless, I continued, taking command of this situation, for was I not mistress of this house? "Surely among our friends—I think of Vuillard, Monet—there are those who would keep your secret and make your stay with us a little richer."

"You were a sweet child and you have grown into a self-possessed woman," said Oscar. "Who was that fellow with you when the panel swung open? Will he present a difficulty?"

"Oh that's only Rilke, Auguste's new secretary," I said with a dismissive wave of the hand. "He didn't see you, and wouldn't recognize you if he did. He speaks very poor French that he learned from Berlitz. He is as timid as a mouse and lives only for Auguste and his own pretentious poetry."

"You seem uncommonly fond of him. Perhaps we had best leave him out of this. Scribblers keep no secrets. What do you say, Auguste?"

"As you will, Oscar. I am old now and I let the younger people run the world." He nodded in my direction. "I work, and I work." Even as he said this the little ball of clay that was always in his hand was being modeled and remodeled by his sure fingers. "It will be good to have you as a guest again. I will do a little portrait of you—without the beard, I think, but otherwise as you now appear. I once did a portrait of my father without his beard and he was very angry with me about it. He felt I had exposed his weak chin."

Oscar smiled. He admired Auguste, who could work and work without constraint. "I have been reading the writings of a man named Sigmund Freud," he said. "Freud would have much to say about the portrait of your father with the weak chin."

It was the kind of statement that men knew enough to let hang in the air, each to ponder in his own way, until the subject returned of its own. I was not so reticent. "What would he say, this Freud man?" I queried.

Oscar paused, cleared his throat. "He would say that in removing your father's beard, Auguste, you had symbolically unmanned him. He would say that your choice to shave his chin was a manifestation of an Oedipal power struggle."

"I don't understand," I said. "What do you mean 'unmanned?'"

"Enough talk!" declared Rodin. "We must leave our visitor some time to rest and change before dinner." He turned to Oscar. "What shall we do about the servants? Some may remember you from your previous visit three years ago."

"If I am called by Francis Canterville, and stay as much from their sight as possible, it is unlikely I shall be recognized. I sat in a third class railway coach from Venice to Paris. During one short stretch of the journey there was a man, a journalist of the foulest nature, who had once blackened my name in England's popular press. I cowered in my disguise when he entered the compartment. I admit, with guilt, that I was pleased to see him reduced to traveling in the lowest class without reservation. He did not recognize me, though his fortune would have been made if he had. I feel quite safe now."

"Then we shall meet again at dinner. Come, ma chérie," said Rodin, taking my arm possessively and leading me from the chamber, sliding the panel shut behind as we left.

"That was a little abrupt," I protested.

"Not so abrupt as this," countered Auguste. He took me violently into his arms and kissed me with passionate intensity. I was distracted for quite awhile from the recovery of my Dear Uncle Oscar. Later when Auguste had returned to his studio and I lolled alone among the sheets, I wondered if the mere proximity of men who love men caused an intensification in the desires of men who love women.

CHAPTER 16

The Memoirs of Aveline Tartine

LA FOLIE NEUFBOURG, PARIS

You will take tea with me now. Tea with the now ancient but still lovely Madame Aveline Tartine, here in the solarium and I will tell you more of Oscar Wilde. I have recently had a bout of illness, but look none the worse for wear. Do you like this kimono of blue silk? A museum would be fortunate to acquire it. Exquisite, yes? Late afternoon sun warms the room, and the doors to the garden are thrown open in consequence. The blend of fresh and hothouse air causes the plants to relax and breathe deeply. I, too, can yet breathe deeply. Life is measured out in breaths (not in English coffee spoons!) And, if you live long enough, you learn that Time is the exhalation of God.

You think my hair, so beautifully styled, may be a wig, yes? Many women of my age do not keep their hair. It becomes thin as well as white, but I have the ancient secrets of great beauty passed on to me by a dear friend. You must guess who this was.

I have before me an unpublished chapter from the unpleasant memoir of the American dancer, Isadora Duncan. What did she call it? Oh, yes…*My Life*…as though no one else was in it! The chapter was first delivered to me many years ago in a hotel in Antibes. Was it 1932? No matter. It was at some time between the wars. I was ripe with beauty then. I asked the hotel clerk as to who had delivered the manuscript, but he looked at me and shrugged helplessly.

Hotel employees are hired for the shortness of their memories. He did notice how lovely I looked, however, and commented on my ensemble. If fine garments are to be of any value one must both wear them and be aware of them. Fully half of a woman's charm is her own awareness of it. Do they teach women nothing nowadays?

I was not amused to receive this chapter. Isadora Duncan! What a chump, to use an American word. From the dawn of the new century I knew everybody who was important—which doesn't mean I liked everybody—and that ridiculous woman, always parading about in her bed sheets or her kitchen curtains, I disliked immensely. Her real name was not Isadora, you know, but plain Dora. She was made up entirely of pretenses. Still, I would not wish tragedy upon her and what tragedies befell her; both of her beautiful little children drowned. Such is the way of Fate that is not cruel, but merely a force destined (fated one might say) to obey the laws of physics without the least regard for human life.

Isadora danced as beautifully as they say. I must give her that, though her extreme exhibitionism was not to my taste. She flaunted her body, as if unaware of its erotic power, while all the time she was observing the attractive men in her audience through half-closed eyes, and counting the money in their pockets as well. She knew how to be a woman.

I know that nowadays women fight for the rights and privileges of men. Why would women want such things? To live like men? Men, they have terrible lives, they do terrible things. They are an oppressed sex; forever making money, supporting families, slaves to their business or their politics or their useless wars where they feel bound to throw themselves onto other men's spears. They know only meaningless sport for pleasure. Their lives are as repetitive as their morning shave. Most go to their graves never having known the sweetness of life.

Except the artists, of course, and women have always been free to be the artist if they wish, yes? Oh she must be strong, that is true, and not care for the reputation, but no matter; reputations are only fictions in the minds of other people, and the minds of other people are as dust. No?

I think now of all those curled up little nuns, there on the other side of the wall who disapproved of all my choices. Now they are laid out straight, in neat little rows with the crosses that mark them beginning to slant and sink into the dirt. Do you care about what was in their minds? Do I? Does anyone? Then go to the museum, Jeu de Paume, and look at one picture painted by Berthe Morisot. Do you think of her reputation? No. You think only of her painting! Morisot was all but spotless, by the way; a dull little woman as women go, but not so dull as Sister Marie-Therese of the Convent of the Sacred Heart!

I lecture. It is the privilege of great age. You listen. It is the privilege of youth. Here, for your instruction is the chapter that came to me. Make of it what you will. The content makes a great anger in me, towards my beloved Auguste, even now. How dared he keep such secrets from me!

⁓ᴈᴠ

An Unpublished Chapter, from
My Life
by Isadora Duncan

My dream could have had no other meaning. My family knew we must leave Oslo immediately and return to Paris. In spite of my success with the students, we had entertained the Norwegian intellectuals so extravagantly with vodka and caviar that we had no money for train fare. My mother was disconsolate, but I wired my many admirers in the city of light and soon the Clan Duncan was situated in two spacious rooms on the Rue de Seine.

As always in Paris our needs were few. Mother, my brother Raymond, my sister Elizabeth, and I would wander in happy delirium for hours in the Louvre. Then, with the appetites of kings, enjoy a simple repast—a bottle of wine, some bread, and a bit of cheese—in the Tuileries or along the banks of the Seine where I would dance a song of appreciation to the chestnut trees, sometimes causing quite a stir amongst the well-buttoned Parisians promenading along the quayside.

On the third day after our return, I went to my friend, Rodin; and, as my dream had foretold, he showed me all the wonderful sculptures on which he was at work and the casts of monuments he had recently completed; the glorious lovers, the smooth skinned women of myth and poetry. I trembled before the mighty Gates of Hell and I was moved to many tears by his great monument of honor, The Burghers of Calais, depicting six brave men, martyred to English sadism. Rodin rendered them as large as life, on their way to tragic death.

After a delicious dinner of roasted chicken and delicate vegetables which we ate together sitting on the studio floor, as though picnicking in a sculpture garden, I was inspired, to Rodin's surprise and delight, to take off my street clothes and don my little white tunic. All through the night, as the moon showered its mystical light down through the skylights, I wove my graceful dance among his masterpieces. It was the wedding night of his genius to mine. After that night I never again danced without the thought of those monumental sculptures waiting for me in the wings.

Towards morning a strange feeling came upon me. I became convinced that we were not alone, that someone was lurking in the shadows of the studio. At last, as dawn began to break the magic spell of the "dark o'erhanging firmament" of night, I knelt at last at the feet of Rodin and rested my weary brow on his knee. He put his great, rough hand upon my head, as the father I had never known might bless a child. But then, through my tears of happiness I saw a figure in the great tableaux, The Burghers of Calais, begin to move. I was amazed as a massive human form detached itself from the group of condemned stone men and walked heavily from the studio. Yet six were still left behind! Rodin, following my frightened gaze, told me it was Oscar Wilde who had watched throughout the night. I was now more frightened than ever for, although I was never simple or silly enough to believe in ghosts, I knew that Oscar Wilde had died some time ago and been buried here in Paris for I clearly recalled how Andre Beauneir, my young admirer who had never become my lover, wept inconsolably as he told me of the death of this great writer.

Auguste said that I must keep a secret at all costs, for united in art as we now forever were, he could keep nothing hidden from me. Oscar Wilde was not dead. It is one of Rodin's sculptures that lies buried in his place in the cemetery. He asked if I would like to meet the infamous writer and I said that I would for I understood he had been a great admirer of all that was beautiful in life. I promised to keep the precious secret and to return the following night.

The next evening I ran through the darkened streets of Paris to the house Auguste had designated. The house was ablaze with the light of a thousand candles.

I was shown into a small dressing room next to the grand dining room by the housekeeper, a woman of frightening aspect. Much to my surprise, she pressed her palm against a mirrored wall and it swung back to reveal a hidden chamber, furnished as a gentleman's study. Before the fireplace Auguste Rodin was sitting with Oscar Wilde. Wilde was a large man whose broken life sat heavily on his brow. Both men were drinking excellent brandy and smoking fine cigars, and they appeared very comfortable with each other as one would not expect, given the differences in their physical appetites. I knew this ease was the true brotherhood of great artists who, with their enlightened minds and ennobled spirits, accept all the varieties of earthly life "and the thousand shocks that flesh is heir to." May the Gods of the future take note!

Both men stood when they saw me come into the room, and Oscar Wilde extended his hand.

"Will you take the hand of a convict made of flesh and blood, my dear? You, who danced so nimbly among the convicts of stone all through the night?"

"All the more willing, Sir, for you were pilloried for love." His hand was as large as Rodin's but soft, and gentle to the touch.

"Where did you find this little treasure, Auguste? For surely she must be the reincarnation of Salomé herself."

He spoke with a calm, mellifluous voice, and I knew I was in the presence of a fine and poetic mind.

"An American," replied Auguste taking my other hand. The two men drew me towards the warmth of the fire, and I felt like a fortunate child being taken for a walk by two adoring parents.

"Yes, of course. I should have known by her spirit and her dress that she could only spring from the American revolutionary soil."

"She will remake the ballet, I believe," said Rodin.

"That won't be at all a bad thing," commented Wilde.

Soon, seated comfortably at their feet with my own glass of brandy in my hand, I felt bold enough to ask of Mr. Wilde why he pretended to be dead when he was really alive. And he said something that I was never to forget, even when I am one hundred years old.

"It is the only way that I can devise to see my own two dear boys as they grow up. They have been taken from me, you know. But from time to time, in a variety of disguises I can spy on them at their play or in their schoolrooms. No one suspects. Not even the children. To see my boys alive, I must be dead. It is a paradox."

I shed tears of sorrow for Mr. Wilde. His own tears he held prisoner behind his penetrating brown eyes.

Many years later, upon the death of my own two small children, I was to remember his words and think how strange it was that if I am ever again to look on the angelic faces of my dearest Dierdre and darling Patrick, I, too, must be dead. And I wished it were so.

But to return to happier recollections. Oscar Wilde was of the impression that he moved in a way that could reveal his disguise. He asked me to teach him how to walk in a less noticeable manner. I have taught many little girls to dance like angels, but had never taught a grown man to walk!

I took his hand and together we moved around the small study, Auguste laughing at our antics, the brandy smoothing our efforts. "You must think of yourself as a God," I told him.

"That is not so very difficult, Miss Duncan," he replied.

"Not mighty Zeus, but lithe Apollo," I corrected him. On we went, and in the end he found the center of his being at last and from there extended first one foot and then the other, balanced and true.

Soon my own footsteps hurried home through awakening Paris, burdened with the secret knowledge that I now possessed, but lightened by my successes with two great men.

CHAPTER 17

Lady Eleanor Ashburton was lying quietly on Dr. Sigmund Freud's rug-covered couch. He sat calmly behind her, where she could not easily see him though the knowledge that he observed the full length of her prone body was, as always, a mildly arousing idea. Nothing but talk, mostly hers, ever occurred between them. She could hear his even breath and smell the ever-present scent of cigar.

"I wonder what you are thinking?" she queried.

He returned the question. "What comes to your mind?"

"About what *you* are thinking? I think you are bored with me, and are thinking of other things entirely, but I don't know what those things may be. I don't know what your interests are. Perhaps you are thinking of a paper you wish to write or what you will eat for your dinner."

"You are confusing me with your distracted father, Lady Ashburton, who always thought of his own interests instead of yours, and who abandoned you at a time in life when you most needed a father's love, following the deaths of your little brother and dear mother."

Eleanora felt the sting of truth in her eyes. She fought back tears. She hated to cry when Freud was watching.

He continued: "You try not to cry. You learned to hide your sadness from your father who disliked womanly displays of feeling, and from your Aunt Gruzella who had no patience with a melancholy child."

Now the tears began to flow without inhibition. She pulled forth from her bodice the lovely lace handkerchief that Timothy had brought her from the Venetian islands and she dabbed away at the cascade.

Freud, she noted, was not restless; he was relentless.

"All your young life you have felt secondary to the interests of those around you. You have constructed your adult life in much the same manner. Even now you feel you are here, with me, in this psychoanalytic treatment, as a second choice, because your friend Oscar Wilde has not come to me. His life and health seem much more important to you than your own."

She listened closely.

"This error is in harmony with what women are taught to want, so you notice nothing pathological in your choices; but in truth this mode of thought—never being first, always being second—is a legacy of your childhood and must be given up."

"But Oscar Wilde is a genius."

"Perhaps he is. Perhaps your brother would also have been so, but do geniuses misfire guns into themselves?"

"Perhaps he was distracted. Perhaps he was thinking of me. I had been cruel to him at breakfast that morning. I had refused to share my strawberry jam."

"So you believe that had you been generous at breakfast, your brother would be alive today. You believe that he covered himself in blood for lack of strawberry jam. This is a child's idea, Lady Ashburton, very grandiose, very powerful to be sure, but not realistic. Your brother is dead of his own carelessness and we will never know the reasons for it."

"Who is to say he was not thinking of me?"

"You cling to your fantasy so tenaciously because it satisfies a romantic notion—that your brother was in love with you and thought only of you even in his dying moment. When, in fact, he was just as likely thinking of a dead fox."

"That is a cruel statement, Dr. Freud."

"Reality is a cruel place, but in it one can live. In a fantasy world, kind as it may be, one can only be half-alive."

"Is our time not up?" Eleanora fought her impulse to bolt.

"Not quite. And I have one other intervention to make before you leave today."

She found herself fearing the interpretation and eager for it at the same time. She had found the experience of analysis dreadful, but also liberating in ways she had not thought possible. During the course of the psychoanalytic treatment she had gained new awareness of herself and her life. She had slowly begun to realize her powers as an original thinker, rather than just an able assistant to others.

"Your fantasy of the strawberry jam, how you withheld it, and unwittingly caused the death of your brother thereby; this fantasy satisfies a deep unconscious wish to have actually killed your brother."

"That is absurd!"

"Is it? He was the elder and favored child, the inheritor—favored, you soon discovered, for the small difference between the legs. You envied him this distinction and wished to kill him."

"You have an abnormal mind, Dr. Freud, to think of such things."

"My mind is not the subject of this analysis. You have lived the unhappy life of a guilty woman, Lady Ashburton, and all your self-punishment has been the consequence of that guilt. Think how you have held yourself back, from marriage, from children, from success of any kind."

"My life has another kind of success."

"Perhaps that is so. But if you could free yourself of this burden of misplaced guilt, how much more would be possible for you? You must understand that your childish wishes were only wishes, not bullets, and they began with the discovery that your physical body was lacking that which society values so much, the penis. If you can admit this, you can free yourself from a life built on envy and guilt." Eleanora felt a slight shift somewhere inside her being. She knew he was right, but at that moment she would rather have died than admit it.

"A woman's body is perfect in its own way, Dr. Freud. It carries and delivers children to the world. Men can only envy our childbearing capacity and try to ape it with their ceaseless striving, their industry, their attempts at invention, their interpretations—"

"Our time is over for today, Lady Ashburton."

"I was just warming to my subject," she protested.

"We have tomorrow."

"Indeed." Without another word she sat up, stood up, and walked with exaggerated dignity from the room.

It was on the stairs that a new thought occurred to her, arriving in her mind with such stunning force that she had to steady herself against the banister for a moment, breathing deeply. She descended the staircase, left the building, and entered on her new life, now entirely changed.

CHAPTER 18

Timothy Tyharde was dining with his father at the battered old kitchen table in the vicarage where he had grown to manhood. The kitchen, like his father, seemed smaller to Timothy, but with that exception everything was just as he remembered it. The iron kettle sat on the sideboard awaiting the next call for tea. The dog, now ancient, slept in a basket pulled up close to the wood-burning stove for warmth. His mother's forlorn collection of ceramic animals lined the window sill over the sink where the light could play upon their smooth backs and chipped noses. How many hours had he watched her moving about the kitchen, uncomplaining, as she served the men who had become her life?

He watched the old man, alone now but for Timothy. He consumed his broth and his bread without thought of conversation. Timothy wondered if the old man's silence over the meal would drive him mad tonight, or if not tonight, then tomorrow night. Had his father, who had once taken a first in Latin, forgotten the meaning of the word *companion?* With whom one breaks bread.

He wondered how men like his father could carry on, day after day, year after year, without any genuine interest in those around them, without variation in their own lives. Routine, he knew, bred a deadening complacency. It had driven Timothy out of the vicarage to London and beyond.

Now he had returned, carrying with him the secret of his own queer nature, and the knowledge of a forbidden love concealed within his breast. What would his father—now dying slowly of accumulated ailments—think of his son had he known of his predilections? Did he know? Timothy would never know.

His father pointed to the salt dish. Timothy, compliant, handed it over to him without a word.

For many years Timothy had known of his difference from ordinary men, his place in the territory of outcast men of every class, united only in their longings for one another. But he had never acted—not until Venice, when he had been Oscar's guest, and fallen a little bit in love in the gondola, and shared one kiss. He had fled first to Paris where he paid a visit to Rodin bringing news of Oscar, and where he met Rodin's charming mistress, Aveline. Then he had gone to Lady Eleanora in Vienna. She had not noticed the slightest difference in Timothy, though he felt himself completely transfigured.

As Eleanora had prattled on about her hopes for Oscar, Timothy had worried about the future of their friendship. If Eleanora found out that Oscar was bestowing kisses on him, not her, she might have a feeling or two about it, and the outcome would not be fine. He loved Eleanora. She had aided his mission house in the East End, not just with money, but also with her influence in high places. Eleanora was all about aid and comfort. Of course, she was different now too, with her new way of looking at life. Psychoanalysis had wrought its changes.

At Oscar's request Timothy had then returned to Venice, feeling both a charge of anticipation and a tremor of trepidation. The combination had been frightful. What, he wondered, would happen if his attraction to Oscar intensified? He had told himself, again and again, that their kiss of the previous visit was but a thing of the night, born of the intimacy of the long, slow glide together in the low, black boat, along the darkened canals towards the dawn. They had gently held hands beneath the small lap blanket, so as not to shock the gondolier, but Timothy's senses had been reeling. Oscar had appeared calm and reflective. It was a prelude.

Timothy had arrived back in Venice in the hot sunlight of afternoon, when all but the tourists and their keepers were asleep. He had used his own key to let himself into the palazzo, and gone directly to the kitchen for water. He was searching in a cupboard for a glass, when someone strongly pulled his arm behind his back and held him fast. Pain shot through his shoulder.

"Who are you? How did you get in here?" demanded an unknown voice. "What are you looking for?"

Had he somehow blundered into the wrong set of rooms? "Release me, you fool!" Timothy protested, and struggled to free himself. "I am a friend of Francis Canterville. Who the devil are you?"

His arm was dropped straightaway and he turned to face his attacker, ready to hurt back. He stayed his hand when he saw that the figure before him was not the brute he had expected, but someone resembling an angel as painted by Piero della Francesca. He could not strike such a marvel whatever the provocation. *Oh, God,* he thought, as awareness dawned. *Oscar has done it again!*

"I'm so sorry," said the young man. "I'm Charles Redfield. I thought you were a burglar, but you must be Mr. Tyharde. Oscar said you were coming, but I didn't realize you had a key."

Timothy's heart dropped further. Oscar had done it again, *and,* like a fool, he was telling the youth everything about his life. Timothy sank down onto a kitchen chair and rubbed his shoulder. His own feelings he noted were mixed: relief that he would not be the object of Oscar's desire, and disappointment.

"Here, let me get you some water," said the beautiful young man, now turned from guardian to ministering angel. "Francis, I mean Oscar, is asleep over a book. Although he says Balzac is his favorite author, his novels work like a sedative on him. I was at work on a new composition when I heard you rustling about in the kitchen. Here." He handed Timothy the glass of water and sat down opposite.

"What kind of composition?" Timothy managed to ask between gulps.

"A piano ballade. Did Oscar tell you I was a composer?"

"Oscar did not tell me about you at all. It's not a musical rendition of *The Ballad of Reading Gaol,* is it?"

"I shall have to leave that sad theme to another. I take my inspiration only from nature. Shall I awaken Oscar?" he asked. "He'll be so glad to see you."

The impetuous young music maker seemed a good enough chap, thought Timothy, and he had best get to know him, in order to assess the danger to their intrigue. "No, let him rest," he replied.

"How is your shoulder?"

"Better." The sharp pain the youth had inflicted was now giving way to a warm, not unpleasant sensation.

"You've known Oscar a long time, haven't you?" asked Charles.

"In sickness and in health," replied Timothy.

"Even death didn't part you. Were you lovers?"

"I beg your pardon!" Timothy was taken aback.

"Oh, sorry. Living with Oscar makes one bold. Please excuse the question."

"No. Let me answer it. It's time I was able to speak of these matters. Oscar and I are not, nor have we ever been lovers. I do love him. I've loved other men, too. But, frankly, I don't engage in the physical aspects of sexuality. I do not feel the need."

"Isn't it wonderful how very different people can be?" responded Charles. "I don't think I was ever anything but physical. I've always found the body thrilling. What I disdain is being dependent on anyone for my happiness, like Oscar was on Bosie. I can jump right into the physical. Then I leave."

Timothy appreciated the boy's candor, but was suddenly worried about further upset to his friend. "Are you going to leave Oscar?"

"I never think I'm going to leave anyone, and then I do. But I'm good at keeping secrets. I won't betray his secret, though I will probably betray him." Charles looked quite sad as he made the prediction about his own behavior.

"Have you prepared him for this?"

"Yes. Oscar is himself unwilling to make another attachment of the heart. He talks about some Gypsy who warned him off such an involvement. Nevertheless, he is a wonderful companion. It is his kindness that draws one closer and closer. Simple, uncalculated kindness."

"He is the best man I have ever known," concurred Timothy. "After his release from Reading Gaol he arranged for money to be sent to prisoners he had met there, and he wrote letters to the *Observer* about the treatment of children in prison. The letters resulted in many reforms. Most men would never have looked back."

As Timothy talked, Charles opened a bottle of Prosecco and set out sweet Italian bread. They were talking, Timothy noted, like a couple of elderly spinsters who had known each other for years.

"His concern for children shows itself here in Venice as well," said Charles. "When he walks the waterfront, he stops at the orphanage to bring treats to the children inside. He gave a little birthday party for a sick child only this week with party hats and little toy horns and a box of cakes. The nuns there don't know what to make of him. At first they were suspicious, of course, but he has quite won them over, and Abate Antonio from the monastery—who disapproves of me, by the way—has vouched for him. More panettone?"

"No, thank you, I'm afraid my tastes run to the plain English digestive biscuit."

Charles leaped to the challenge, producing an assortment of English biscuits from a tin in the cupboard. Timothy found his consideration charming, and he was beginning to feel the wine. "You know, I may not care for Italian sweets but this Prosecco makes me feel quite cheerful."

"I'm pleased," said Charles. "After that awful reception I gave you." He reached out and caressed Timothy's shoulder.

There was something in the gentle gesture of concern that moved Timothy. He remembered his mother's caresses, soft as the breath of a cat on his head, his cheek, his shoulder, his back. "Oscar has done well to find you, Charles, and he would do well to keep you."

"That will not be possible," declared an unexpected voice, and they turned to see Oscar in the doorway. He was smiling, resplendent in a Turkish caftan of purple silk with golden trim.

Both men started to speak at once, but Oscar raised a silencing hand. His entrance was not yet complete. He moved swiftly across the kitchen, first to take Timothy's hand, then to pour himself a glass of wine, which he both savored and swallowed at once. Then he spoke again: "It will not be possible to keep dear Charles, for he is a will o' the wisp when it comes to love. That is his charm. I never know when I awaken if he will be there by my side or flown to another." He looked knowingly at Timothy for a moment.

"But surely Oscar, you don't think—" began Timothy.

"Tim," Oscar interrupted, "these matters do not require thought." He reached over and touched Timothy's shoulder just as Charles had done. Clearly he had been watching from the shadows of the next room. "Now does that feel the same as Charles's gentle touch?"

"More or less," replied Timothy. He was both fascinated and repelled by the turn of events.

"More truth, Tim," Oscar challenged.

"All right then, Oscar, and be damned. It felt entirely different."

"Then where shall we dine?"

"Let me prepare the dinner, Oscar." It was Charles, already on his feet and moving about the kitchen.

"It's bad enough that he insists on writing the most divine music, but he is a wizard with victuals as well. The maid wept with envy after sampling his prawn bisque. I quite despair of his ever being useless enough to succeed in good society."

Oscar put an arm around Timothy's shoulders. "Let us leave Charles to his labors," he suggested, leading Timothy, captive in the strong arc of his arm, swiftly into the drawing room. Once they were alone he flung open the shutters. Outside, the first breath of evening air lightened the thickness of the afternoon haze.

"He's delightful, isn't he Tim? I so wanted you to meet him. Good looking and brimming with talent. You know, there will come a time in England when a shopkeeper's son will court a princess, when a white man will serve at table to a black, and when a man will love another man without disgrace, but for now our Charles must be kissed in secret if he is to have the brilliant future he deserves."

"And here you are, the very embodiment of discretion," commented Timothy dryly.

Oscar paused. "Dear Tim, what passed between the two of us was a stolen moment. One perfect kiss while the gondolier busied himself with his pole. Lovely was it not?"

"You speak of that night so easily."

"A clear conscience can bear many pleasures."

"I am afraid that this vicar's son has a conscience the consistency of prawn bisque," said Timothy ruefully.

"You are a good man, Tim. Unfortunately, like all good men, you are quite wicked to yourself. Why, if you treated others as you do yourself, you would be thought the meanest man in town. Now you must clear your thoughts of self-condemnation and accept who you are, and whom you are destined to love. And while you are at it you must not be jealous about Charles. I have purchased him at great expense to Eleanora, expressly for you."

"Whatever do you mean—for me? Charles is in love with you."

"Charles is unable to form a truly lasting relationship with any of his lovers. It's not at all good for him and he knows it. I have entrapped him for a brief while with the help of Venice. He takes the water and air and stone of this place as his muse—"

"I think he is here entirely for what you bring to him."

"Well, I do have a splendidly appointed kitchen, and that plays into it. But you know, Tim, I am a wanderer myself now. When you sign on for love in this world, you sign on for suffering, and I have had my share of both. I want someone solid to take Charles in hand, to settle him down so he can work at his compositions steadily. There is celestial music in the boy. He will need the fire of love for that music to flare forth from within his soul."

"I still don't see where I come into it."

"I was thinking that you might marry Charles, so to speak. Some men can do this kind of thing; settle in, nest for life, with someone they love."

"You are talking nonsense!" declared Timothy.

"One man's nonsense is another man's law. Think it over, Timothy: a good antique emporium in a continental city would suit you. It's not a gentlemen's life, of course, but with a beautiful suite of rooms to come home to, music in the background, delectable food in the dining room, Charles in the bedroom, it is a life to consider. Otherwise you may end your days in your own soup kitchen—albeit on the better end of the ladle—or get sucked back to dreary Scotland, and that would be a great pity."

"And how would I finance this idyllic venture, even if I were tempted?"

"Eleanora would help. She's already written that she would. And you have an eye for beauty, Tim, a heart for authenticity. Your shop would soon flourish."

"You two! You and Eleanora, conspiring to give me another life than the one I have chosen. It's patronizing and utterly absurd!"

"Didn't you and Eleanora conspire to give me this life? Is it not absurd? But does it not hold promise? You and I and Eleanora always conspire. We conspire together for one another. We are true friends, Timothy, and friends are God's apology for family."

It was then that Timothy did the most unlikely thing he had ever done. He threw his arms around Oscar, burying his face in the man's broad chest. Oscar returned the embrace. "I am so glad you are alive," Timothy murmured, "so glad."

"And I, you."

"Dinner is served," announced Charles who had stepped into the drawing room unseen.

His father interrupted Timothy's recollections. The old vicar pushed back his empty soup bowl and awkwardly made his way to the stove. He returned with a plate of boiled chicken and potatoes that had been left simmering by the village girl who did for him. Timothy's own soup bowl had been empty for some time, but he had no appetite for boiled chicken. He was longing for prawn bisque, and for Charles.

CHAPTER 19

The Memoirs of Aveline Tartine

We must turn our attention to Lord Alfred Douglas. Bosie, they called him. A silly name for a silly man. Lord Alfred Douglas was a poor specimen of his sex, the son of a madman. He lived a long life for a man of so small a character. It is often the way. Bitterness is a strong tonic.

Bosie died just after the second big war, in 1945. He was an unpleasant old man by then, trying always to write the poetry but in the main only causing trouble to other men's lives. Did you know he libeled Winston Churchill? Yes.

In print he criticized his strategies at the Battle of Jutland. Churchill brought suit and won. Bosie Douglas finally went to prison himself for libel. There he wrote *In Excelsis,* a match for Oscar's *De Profundis.* Freud would make much of it. No?

Why did Oscar forever love Bosie Douglas? I think there is always one, amidst however many others, one who endures. For me, of course, it was Auguste Rodin. I come now at times to the secret study to think of him, so long away from me, so soon to return. I shall bring some order to his heavenly existence, yes? To his little white cloud.

Look here at this place, at the walls of the study, do you see nothing unusual? This strange wallpaper…the rows of seeming texture, the horizontal bars and the vertical? Look closer. They are all the books of this library, turned wrong side in. Oscar did this thing in his spare hours here.

It was a parlor trick of his to select any requested volume from the rows of shelves...though the spines were hidden.

I've often thought that Oscar got the idea for the reversal of the books from Vuillard in whose paintings people melt in and out of wall textures. Or perhaps Vuillard took his ideas from Oscar, who took wallpaper with utmost seriousness. Oscar liked Vuillard's paintings and his quiet companionship as well; and he felt a strong affinity with Monet, particularly Monet's love of flowers.

Yes, Monet was here in the secret study, and Wilde went once or twice to Giverny. Wilde did not care much for the Impressionists in general—he preferred the Nabis, would have loved the Fauves—but he attributed a general improvement in the look of the French countryside to the efforts of the Impressionists. He declared that man could only appreciate in nature what he has first been exposed to in art. You agree, yes? He was convinced that Monet's use of new colors one autumn would cause new flowers to appear in the spring. How confining this windowless room must have seemed to him, though he never complained.

Once I tried to save him from tedium and almost ruined his life again. Then, I was young. And Oscar forgave anyone young.

CHAPTER 20

O scar was contemplating the wall of books. He had, over the course of his lifetimes, read almost all of them, the Balzacs several times. Perhaps, he thought, his tragedy was that he was never certain as to whether he wished to be Balzac himself or one of his characters. He thought of the trap door he had been shown in Balzac's house that led down into the wine caves where the old scribbler escaped from the din of his creditors. His eyes moved about over the parquet floor of Rodin's secret study. There was no discernible trap door. He knew, in fact he had often said, that there was no greater sin in life than to be bored, but he was.

Patience kindly offered to be of help to him if he would let her. "Oh, go away," he muttered aloud. He knew what he needed to do. He needed to write. He had thought when he found Charles Redfield on that delightful evening in Venice, that his muse might be returning, but it had turned out to be Charles' muse instead, resulting in the most glorious music issuing forth from the palazzo.

Charles had said it was the light and the water, constantly moving without a care for time or melody, that compelled him to bring both into being, but Oscar knew it was love. Love too, had no respect for time, had no care for those who listened to its ceaseless murmur. Love goes its own way as surely as light and water.

When Charles had left him Oscar had been relieved, and he had been relieved at his relief, for it meant that life was not going to replay itself with an obsession over another young man.

The decampment of Charles Redfield had given him just the reason he needed for another change of air. He had rowed out to the Isola to say his farewells to the Abate and the brothers and, if truth be known, to the birds. He genuinely missed Hector. And, he admitted to himself, he missed Abate Antonio too, a man who had made such a careful study of Oscar's writing that he could quote entire scenes, rather like scripture. Fra Ricardo, and Paul, and the other friars had prayed over him, as they did before each of his journeys, captive as they were to their vow to remain only upon the little island. How do they do it? Oscar wondered. Prudence, said Prudence.

"Oh, do shut up!"

Just then he heard a familiar rap at the panel. "Come in little squirrel," he called, pleased with the distraction.

Aveline entered in a lovely mauve frock, knowing it to be Oscar's favorite color. "Have you been talking to yourself?" she queried. "I thought I heard you as I approached the panel."

"When one converses with oneself one has the assurance of attention."

"I have an idea, Dear Uncle Oscar."

"One of us was bound to have one sooner or later."

"We could go for a carriage ride. It's a splendid day. Everyone in Paris is out. We should be, too."

"Oh, but you know it depresses me to be all closed up inside a carriage when everyone else is in an open fiacre or strolling about en plein air. It has become easier for me to retreat entirely than to go about in a cage with wheels."

"But you haven't heard the idea yet. If you dress up in women's clothing—there's plenty about from Auguste's old mistresses—you could go as my Auntie. We might even have a picnic in the Bois de Boulogne. It would be such fun."

"Your Great Auntie?" queried Oscar, humoring her along for the moment. "You told me you had no relations."

"And you told me to acquire some."

"Well dressing up in other people clothing does lead to plot development, if not to character development. See Shakespeare on the subject."

"You're to go as a great lady," she announced.

"But I haven't worn women's garments since I was a child. My mother used to cut down her old dresses for me. It was the fashion in those days. Quite a pretty fashion. But now, with my great height, we should have to cut the dresses up, not down."

"It doesn't matter. I shall love cutting them up. I was going to burn them but this is much better. We can sew two together if need be, and much can be done with flounces and shawls. We'll make you look like a very beautiful, imposing dowager."

"With a beard."

Aveline crossed her arms and surveyed Oscar's face with a pretty pout. "The beard will have to go, of course. And unlike Auguste's father, you have a very strong chin, so you won't mind."

"Prudence tells me this is a very bad idea, Aveline. Perhaps we should have a picnic here in the garden instead. You could send the gardener out on some entrancing and lengthy errand, to buy a new hoe, or whatever it is that gardeners buy."

"No. It's a carriage ride that you need, down the grand boulevards."

"In skirts?"

"In skirts."

"Well, if it will amuse you Aveline. Now where are these shrewish garments? I was once regarded as an authority on the subject of women's fashion."

"How can that be? No man would know of such things. I think you are making to joke at me."

"I do not make jokes. I was the editor of a London magazine called *Women's World.*"

She looked skeptical, so he continued.

"Truly. I wrote of all things fashionable and tried in so doing to make the world a more beautiful place."

"And the English women, they listened to you?"

"Indeed they did. Everyone was after my fashion. Why all the P.B.s would put on their prettiest dresses and then worry most piteously about what Oscar Wilde would think of them."

"P.B.s?" she queried.

"Professional Beauties."

"These professional beauties, they are the fallen women of London? No?"

"I dare say some had fallen quite a long way or had hopes of doing so. But no, they were society women, famous for their breeding and their beauty, much like race horses, trotted out for English gentlemen to admire."

"Did they appeal to you?"

"When I was young they most certainly did. At rather great expense I maintained friendships with many of the famous women of my time, the professional beauties and the great actresses too: Lillie Langtry and Sarah Bernhardt, Ellen Terry, and in America, Mary Anderson. And they all looked to me for their style. I wrote a poem to Ellen Terry upon seeing her Ophelia, in which I called her a 'wan lily over-drenched with rain.' She quite liked the phrase."

"Did you ever want to be a beautiful woman?"

"Why you audacious imp! What a question. No," declared Oscar. "But I would have liked to be a beautiful man. Beauty was not my gift. Still, with my charm I could attract beautiful people around me and I gazed at them in lieu of a mirror."

"Have you noticed that you have now become a beautiful man?"

Oscar brightened. "Do you think so, Aveline? That's a very kind thing to say."

"And Auguste will sculpt a beautiful bust of you. Yes?"

"Well, my looks will surely improve when the sculpture is done."

"And you have learned to walk with grace."

"And no one on whom to bestow it."

"Must gifts be given away?"

"I have always tried to do so, and I must have been a great success at it for I have nothing left to give."

"You have accepted me and liked me from the first moment we met. It gave me confidence to find my place here with Auguste."

"So I have been influential in turning a gawky child into a lovely woman so Rodin can turn her into a mistress and then into a beautiful statue. I have played merry with Pygmalion."

"Now it is my turn to play. I will turn you into a lovely woman, too.

I'll bring the dresses and the sewing things here while you shave. Dear Uncle Oscar, you will so much enjoy the day in the sunshine!" And out through the panel she slid.

Oscar smiled. What would Dr. Freud make of all this? he mused, as he got out his shaving kit.

In a short time the transformation had been accomplished. Aveline's great auntie wore grey as befitted her widowed state, with a matching hat and veil. The lavender gloves she carried were her one concession to folly. Shoes, of course, were impossible, but as the two ladies were to stay in the carriage until a secluded place of disembarkation could be found, her men's boots would have to remain hidden beneath her voluminous skirts. Aveline had sent Madeleine to rent a suitable carriage, knowing the maid would choose one with a driver she fancied, and her flirtations kept the man distracted while Aveline and great auntie settled themselves in the sunlit conveyance.

"Whistler should be alive to paint us," whispered Oscar. "We are an étude in gray and mauve."

"Who is Whistler?" asked Aveline.

"You have just made my day, little squirrel," said Oscar. He rapped his walking stick on the floor of the carriage to signal the driver onward.

The ring of the horses' hooves across the cobblestones struck Oscar as a superb sound after the long days of silent contemplation and quiet conversation. Aveline was having a delightful time watching the passersby watching them.

They appeared to notice nothing out of the ordinary about the two grand ladies, except perhaps the stylish angle of their bonnets.

Aveline had instructed the driver to take them down the Champs-Élysées in the direction of the Bois de Boulogne, and it was there that the impossible happened.

They were stopped at a cross street and great auntie was telling her niece about a carriage accident she had endured on this very boulevard many years ago, when suddenly she stopped speaking in mid-sentence. Her large, smooth jaw dropped and for a moment her mouth of fine ivory-white teeth was left wide open in shock.

"What is it? What is it?" cried Aveline. "What is wrong dear Uncle… dear Auntie?"

"Look there!" Oscar was as white as his teeth.

"Where? What?" Aveline could see nothing unusual.

"It's Bosie. Lord Alfred Douglas. There at the café."

Indeed a once beautiful, now handsomely dissipated creature was staring at the carriage from his seat on the boulevard.

"He is looking at us with intensity."

"He is looking at you," corrected Aveline.

"Why does he stare so?"

"Because you are looking at him. But he cannot recognize you. He recognizes only your interest in him, and he is like a bee to honey drawn."

"I must go to him," declared Oscar.

"You are wearing a dress."

"Oh God, of course I can't reveal myself to him as I am. I have endured scandal, but skirts? Aveline, whatever am I to do? My heart is thundering." He had recovered his color. Indeed, he had gone quite red in the face. Aveline had never before seen him at such a loss.

"What do you *want* to do?" she asked him.

"Tell the driver not to proceed. I must consult my inner life."

"Stay here at the crossroads for one moment," commanded Aveline, who liked giving commands.

Oscar was stripping off his lavender gloves, and for a moment Aveline imagined that he would tear off the rest of his clothing and dash off to Bosie in his underwear. But having revealed his own hand, he stared hard at his palm.

"What are you doing?" demanded Aveline.

"I am reading a note that I once left for myself in the event of this particular emergency. See? Here. That nexus of fine lines. Now be quiet." He continued to ponder the pattern that nature had left on his palm.

"Driver!" he said suddenly in his perfect French. "Drive on. Drive on as if your life depends upon it."

The driver cracked his whip and the carriage lurched into motion, barely missing one of the new horseless carriages that was making its noisome way across the intersection.

"No!" It was Oscar, crying out again. "Stop. Please stop, for the love of God." The driver, frightened by the urgency, and confusion of commands, instead cracked the whip again, and the carriage plunged away down the boulevard. Oscar began to weep. "Go back, go back," he pleaded.

"We cannot go back, dear Uncle Oscar," whispered Aveline. "Never, never, never can we go back."

The moment was past. Oscar, reduced to a heap of veils and tears, slumped against Aveline's shoulder and sobbed quietly.

"Why do you weep so?" she asked him tenderly.

"He looked so very sad to me. So lost. He always did, I suppose. I wished only to make him happy. Only that."

"But this is an impossible wish. We cannot make the happiness of others. You know this surely. Yes?"

"What one knows and what one wishes seldom meet. And why is it impossible—with all we know, with all we feel—why is it impossible to make one another happy?"

"Because each of us brings our unhappiness up with us from childhood. We do not relinquish it easily, certainly not to suit another's fancy, for it is part and parcel of who we are. You want to make someone happy. Make a child happy. It is your only hope."

"How do you know this, Aveline? You are but a child yourself."

"Perhaps that is why. I know what I felt, such a short time ago, there in the convent. I was a lonely, sad child. I am not so very different now, deep inside myself, in spite of all my acquisitions and all my accomplishments."

"Perhaps Dr. Freud is right."

"I never understand you when you talk of this Dr. Freud."

"You most intuitively do."

Oscar was wiping his eyes on a lace handkerchief, and was about to blow his nose when Aveline restrained him. "A lady does not do that in public."

"Quite. What the devil do you do?"

"Each lady has her own tricks."

He snorted.

She laughed.

"That was not very graceful," he admitted. "There. I'm over the worst of the shock."

"A good meal and good wine will comfort you. We are almost to the edge of the forest. I will send the driver in search of a secluded place to lay out our picnic, and then we will eat and drink and rest."

"Like a painting by Manet."

"No. No. By Renoir," Aveline protested, laughing. "I will not take off my clothes in the woods as Manet suggests."

"What a delightful creature you are. I shall hate to leave you."

"Leave me? Why would you be leaving me?"

"The sight of Bosie Douglas compels me to flee. Knowing he is here, in Paris, will make my solitude unbearable. It is time I visited the Lady Eleanora Ashburton who is in Vienna. She insists in every letter. The change will do me good or ill, as the case may be."

"Then my idea it was of no use," said Aveline with disappointment.

"Your idea, like all ideas, led us to the unforeseen. But cheer up, my squirrel, I have brought apricot cakes in this box and you shall have them all."

Aveline reached eagerly for the cakes, then paused. "What did you read in your palm?"

He did not answer the question. She could see he was back at the crossroads again, looking at Bosie.

"Did you see what he had in his hands?" he asked. There was much distress in his voice.

"A drink. It is not too early to have a drink. No?"

"Yes, the drink I excuse, but he was reading a racing paper. He, who was made for poetry pores over a tout sheet like a stupid fool. And did you see his eyes?"

"Yes. They were fixed on you."

"There is a look I learned in prison. A man may be suffering, but he has not the look. A man may be near death, but he has not the look. But when a man has been driven mad, silently and privately mad, he has it.

You look into the eyes and you see that all kindness, all compassion, all warmth has been extinguished. Bosie has the look."

He sighed deeply. Aveline patted the back of his hand.

"How strange is it," he mused, "here in the year of our Lord, 1904, that old and ruined Oscar Wilde is alive, and the beautiful, young Bosie Douglas is all but dead."

"It is only a fancy, Dear Uncle Oscar. A horrid fancy."

"Is it?" he asked.

CHAPTER 21

The Memoirs of Aveline Tartine

I remember it well. It was a melancholy picnic in spite of the apricot cakes. And he left La Folie the very next day. He strongly feared a collapse of will, a return to Bosie Douglas. So now you have heard about— what do you say in America?—the short haircut? No? The close shave.

I have a little place in the history books. Now you agree, yes? For it was I, Aveline Tartine, who prevented the final reunion of Oscar Wilde and Lord Alfred Douglas.

Voilà!

So here now I present you with a note and a letter, both written by Bosie Douglas himself, both addressed to Oscar's friend and literary executor, Robert Ross. There is a photograph, too, though I cannot understand how Bosie Douglas got hold of it for I took it myself. These things were sent to me from London in, I believe, 1913.

> To Robert Ross from Lord Alfred Douglas
>
> Two copies of the attached document exist: the copy enclosed herein which I send for your perusal and displeasure, and the original document which I have given as a gift to the English speaking world in the care of the Library of Congress in the United States of America with instructions that it not be unsealed until the year 2022.
>
> Regards, Bosie

Letter addressed to the Public of the next millennium, in the care of the Library of Congress, United States of America:

As the whole world knows I, Lord Alfred Douglas, was an especial friend of Mr. Oscar Wilde from several years before his downfall in London until the known end of his depraved life in Paris in 1900. Indeed I was the chief mourner at his funeral.

Many silly things have been written about me and Mr. Wilde among them that I was in some way a part of, or responsible for, the vicious activities that led to his disgrace. It would be preposterous for me to further defend myself, more than I have already been forced to do in response to the excerpts read out in open court from the manuscript known (ridiculously, I might add) as *De Profundis,* which the villainous Wilde wrote in a seizure of gaolhouse madness as a personal letter to me and which I never received, and which was later stolen from me by Robert Ross.

Therefore, I will let my previously published books speak against these cowardly accusations, as a gentleman is bound to do in the interests of his descendants and for posterity, for which I do not care a tuppence.

In this document, however, I will expose yet another of the nefarious deeds accomplished by the "well-meaning" coterie of friends who surrounded Wilde at the time of his disgrace and final illness. It is a secret so black, so heartless, that it will forever end the cult of Wilde worshipers, if any such deluded souls exist at the turn of the next century.

The truth seems next door to impossible when put down in plain King's English, but it is so, and I say it to be the truth that Oscar Wilde did not die at the Hôtel d'Alsace in the year 1900; nor is he buried in Père Lachaise Cemetery under that hideous monument as believed by all and sundry. Some other man or thing lies in his supposed grave.

Oscar Wilde lived on for many years and his final resting place is unknown.

Yes, it is true that Oscar Wilde was spirited away from his deathbed. Although I paid all the bills for Wilde's funeral and burial this deception was not revealed to me until fully five years later and under circumstances that have secured my silence during my lifetime and the lifetime of my son. (But let us call a spade a spade: the spade being blackmail.)

Wilde, as I will prove, lived on under the name of Francis Canterville—a cheap reference to one of his silly stories—in Venice, Vienna and Paris, with occasional trips to Scotland and to seaside resorts.

Why, you may ask, was his anonymity villainy? We can begin with the horror and grief, which were felt unnecessarily upon his "death" by those who cared for him.

But this evil is small compared with the deprivation to his sons of his fatherly interest and involvement, and this is the unforgivable crime which, as a father myself, I know a great deal about. It matters not in the end how harsh or how shameful was the father, how unfilial the son. Reconciliation is all, such as I had with my own father on his deathbed, and as a result of which he left me all of his estate that was possible, under British law, to arrange.

But we would not expect such enlightenment from a man like Wilde. As much as I, in my youthful delusion, cared for the man, I am not, nor will I ever be blind to his faults, which were many and grievous. I have, if the truth were known, forgiven him everything, including the blackening of my good name which has ruined my life and cost me hundreds of pounds in various writs of restraint and libel suits; but this last infamy, this false demise, is very taxing even to a kind and forgiving heart such as my own.

If I had been privy to his whereabouts I would have gone to him, fallen to my knees, and begged for an end to the shameful deception. I would have led him back to a life in the sun, to his writing (for which I was, in past times, more than a little responsible), and to the conviviality which was available to even so fallen a man as he. But his terrible acquaintances did not afford me this opportunity. They kept him hidden from me and from all well-meaning gentlemen, secreted like a big fat spider in a web of lies that will shock and disgust the world when it is fully revealed.

I know for a fact that they were mainly frogs and artists.

Rilke, the pretentious Austrian poet, knew, and the mad-woman Isadora Duncan. Englishmen, who know themselves not to be gentlemen, conspired as well; among them, Timothy Tyharde and George Bernard Shaw, who is not English, but Irish like Wilde himself so perhaps we can expect little else from the likes of him.

So we have all been duped, but the biggest dupe is Oscar Wilde himself who consented to the sham death and the sham life. I can only conjecture that the loss of his fame was too much for him to bear and without his laurel wreath, which was the only garment he really cared about for all his fripperies and fol-derol, without this wreath of acclaim he felt he could no longer be seen in public. Poor Oscar Wilde.

But enough of poor Oscar Wilde! It is a pretty thing when a man, even a disgraced man, must hide his own existence.

Attached herein is a photograph taken in Paris in the year 1906. The automobile in the background can prove this. It is certainly and in every way a likeness of Mr. Wilde that I, as the person who once knew him best (except, of course, for his hidden viciousness) can swear to be him. How I came to possess this photograph will be my secret unto the grave.

Why, you may ask, if I am innocent of Wilde's vices, do I not submit this photograph to the press? Why do I remain silent until the next century? I can answer that in a twinkling. I am tired of the endless hounding by blackguards and yellow journalists, particularly those who have in hand certain letters of my youth that the idiotic public would be pleased to mis-interpret. For myself I care not...but for my son, I would lay down my very life. So what is a small silence on his behalf? We all make the mistakes of youth. Let him make his own, so say I. And if he does so, he will eat his gruel with a short spoon, as I have done.

By the year 2022 when this letter sees the light of day, Wilde's literary reputation will be seen for the poor thing it is, and this revelation of mine will be but a minor curiosity. Still, let it be said that the monstrous remains monstrous even after its own death. History will judge who was the better man, Wilde or I.

I for one shall not abate my opinion one jot or tittle.

Yours, always the better man,
LORD ALFRED DOUGLAS

You see? It is as I, Madame Aveline Tartine, have said. Bosie Douglas was a perfect fool.

CHAPTER 22

Eleanora was asleep at her desk, with her books for a pillow when Oscar tapped lightly on her shoulder.

"Whatever are you doing?" he whispered.

It was the sound of his voice, not the gentle touch that startled her into consciousness.

"Oscar! What a surprise? What happened to your beard? You look so yourself."

"I must do something about that at once. I don't want to go about looking like myself. It's so expected of one. But speaking of appearances, whatever are you wearing?"

"Black."

"Yes, it is black. If it were just black, you would be my black swan, but that is a man's black suit. Are you in mourning for George Sand?"

"No," she said rubbing her eyes.

"Are you intending to *be* the next George Sand?"

"No. The next psychoanalyst, I hope."

"Good God."

"There is no God. God is just a comforting fantasy," she said dismissively.

"I've never found the idea of God the least bit comforting." He shook his head in mock ruefulness. "How you have changed, my Swan. You don't wish to become the ugly duckling do you?"

"Oh, Oscar. There is so much to tell you. I didn't want to put it into a letter, but I've found myself."

"You never seemed lost to me, Eleanora. You always seemed as well founded as anyone I knew. A psychoanalyst? Do they all cross-dress? What a peculiar profession it must be. I have had an adventure by way of that particular perversion myself lately. I'll tell you all about it at some calmer moment."

He looked around the fashionably appointed room, hung with the new Viennese paintings, recognizing Gustav Klimt and Egon Schiele. "And, come to think of it, why on earth do you need a profession? Have I managed to spend all your spare pocket inheritance?"

"It's not for the money, Oscar. I've heaps of money. It's because I love psychoanalytic theory so much. I love having a mind and knowing more and more about it. I lived the first half of my life in utter unconsciousness. And I was lonely, too. No one seemed to understand me, least of all myself. And now it is all coming clear. Dr. Freud is a genius! Of course, you are too, dear Oscar. But of an entirely different sort."

"Loquaciousness in a woman just aroused from her slumber is very becoming."

"Aroused from slumber! The phrase, exactly. Leave it to you, dear Oscar. I have been aroused from slumber." With that she jumped up and gave Oscar an unabashed kiss on the mouth, accompanied by an embrace that brought her entire body into contact with his own. "I've been longing to do that for years," she exclaimed. She kissed him again.

"Your Dr. Freud has a liberating effect on you, my dear," Oscar managed to comment, between kisses. He was enjoying the soft curves of flesh pressed upon his lips, her pliant body sensed, more than felt, through the layers of his suit and hers. "I am a champion of liberation, but are you sure you are quite all right?"

"I have never in my life been better," she declared happily. "I wear what I want, and eat what I want, and sleep when I want, and kiss whom I choose. Lady Caldwell-Allen refuses even to visit."

"Don't tell me you have taken to kissing Lady Caldwell-Allen!"

"One would fear for one's lips. No, she is scandalized by the way I now live and dress."

"Whatever would your Great Auntie Gruesome say?"

"But I don't care, Oscar. I am a separate being. I have indeed been liberated from all conventional thought. Why, do you know I sometimes take off all my clothes and pose for Egon Schiele?" She paused, then corrected herself. "Not quite *all* my clothes, actually, though I would prefer it. He has a fetish for petticoats. I believe it results from a childhood glimpse up his mother's skirts."

"And you are to become a psychoanalyst, and work these licentious wonders on other unsuspecting mortals?"

"The idea came to me as I was leaving a particularly difficult session with Dr. Freud. Of course, I must grasp the theory entire, and be able to use the technique to Sigmund's satisfaction."

"Sigmund, is it now? How you move from icon to icon. It quite takes ones breath away. You are a marvel, Eleanora, a marvelous marvel."

"Let us have a drink to celebrate your arrival," she suggested.

"At six in the morning? Is it not a little late in the day for tippling?"

"For champagne?"

"You are quite right. It is the best possible hour for champagne. It is always the best possible hour for champagne. Have you any *figs?*"

"This is Vienna, not Venice, but I'll have one of the boys go for wild strawberries." She spoke rapidly into a horn mounted onto the wall, giving exact instructions.

"The boys?" Oscar was curious.

"Now don't be envious, Oscar. I have several boys who serve me. All as beautiful as Gods."

"You know, Eleanora, from outside on the Philharmoniker Strasse these rooms look like any proper and wealthy Austrian abode. I expected none else but long draperies and longer faces inside. What a surprise to discover a den of purest iniquity. What has happened to the Lady Eleanora Ashburton of the past? Where are her stays and corsets? Prudence is struck dumb."

"All gone, Oscar. I never cared for the rules, as you know, or you wouldn't be here now. They are naught but the constructions of other, duller people. The only good they serve is to keep society grinding along at a snail-like pace, the only pace that the majority of people can manage. Society's rules hold me no longer, as you see." She popped the champagne cork as if she had been popping and pouring all her life.

"But I still love you, Oscar, with all my heart. That will never change." He lifted his glass to her. "It is a pleasure, you know, to take the unflappable Oscar Wilde aback. Admit that I have quite startled you."

"You have, my dear, you have indeed, and 'twas I that thought to catch you unawares."

As they sipped the champagne, a handsome young man, barefoot and wearing an earring, brought them the tiny red strawberries, powdered with fine sugar. She shot an interested glance towards Oscar who was pleased to return it, and then slipped quietly away.

"I couldn't write this, Eleanora," Oscar commented between sugary bites. "Were I to put a character through such a transformation, no reader would believe it—except perhaps in a fairy tale. Everyone believes everything in fairy tales."

"But would your fictional character have undergone a deep psychoanalysis with the master himself? That is the ticket to transformation."

"I've sampled Freud's writings as you've sent them along. I certainly didn't know psychoanalysis uncorked Victorian-bred ladies like so many bottles of champagne."

"Psychoanalysis will uncork the world," she declared.

"Then the world will be a better place."

"Oh, I do hope so, Oscar. The world is so grim as it is. Look what happened to you, and all for ignorance."

"I did it for love," he whispered.

"I'm sorry, Oscar. I didn't mean to imply that you were ignorant, only that society, high and low, was and is. And you must admit that even love gets overhung with fantasy—the vine of fantasy, choking off its host."

"But that is what a lover is for, my Swan, to provide a convenient chaise longue for our fantasies to drape themselves upon. I saw him not long ago, Eleanora. He who was both vine and host to me."

"Bosie? How sad," was all she said.

"How do you know it was sad?" he queried. "Perhaps it was an enchanting reunion under the star-spangled counterpane of a nighttime sky."

"That would be a psychological impossibility. About as likely as your falling in love with me."

Oscar raised an eyebrow and took a small sip of champagne. He set the glass down with delicacy. "You speak directly these days, Eleanora," he said. "But is not the first duty of a gentleman to dream? To dream of impossible beauty and impossible love? Should there not be a place for both reality and fantasy in this flat world of imagined roundness?"

"Only if the gentleman can tell the difference between the two."

"Can you?" he challenged.

"Yes," she declared, "though Freud has been hinting lately that I cannot."

"A great man who hints? That seems very unlikely to me, very unlikely," Oscar teased.

"You know what I mean, Oscar." She pursed her lips and shook her head as if to clear it. "No. No. Of course, you don't. You've never been on the couch. I must remember who is analyzed and who is not. Let me explain." Again, she paused in consternation. "Oh I cannot! It's a pity that psychoanalysis is so like a religion. One comprehends it or one doesn't. Like having faith or not having faith, though psychoanalysis is opposed to faith…"

Oscar was enjoying her effusions. It reminded him of long ago conversations on warm spring nights, in Oxford rooms lit only by candles, with pretty boys in the first blush of intellectual pleasures.

Eleanora sighed. "I can't explain it. But…well…I think Freud thinks that I have imagined you."

"That's the cleverest thing you've said about him yet. Let's see, how does it go? Freud fantasizes that you have fantasized me. Does he imagine you wrote my plays as well? And my poems? Have you thought up my elegant style in matters of fashion? No wonder you wear such a finely cut suit!"

She shook her head in mock dismay. "No. I haven't explained it properly. Let me try again." She could see that Oscar was amused at the mare's nest she was making of Freudian theory. A sudden thought occurred to her: He probably understands it far better than I do; Freud would not get past him for long. "Freud doesn't think I made you up altogether. He grants that you lived the life you lived."

"Very small of him, I must say," declared Oscar.

"But," she continued, "he thinks I imagined the whole part about saving you from your deathbed, and the Isola, and Venice, the Abate, and Tim, and Charles, and Rodin's secret chambers in Paris, and what's her name? I always have trouble with that name...the chestnut tart, Aveline Tartine, and Vuillard and Monet coming to visit you there, and all the rest."

"Would that you had written it, my dear Eleanora. What a curiosity it would be!"

"Except for this encapsulated psychosis—that is the technical name for it—he thinks that I am quite sane, and gifted in the ways of psycho-analytic thought."

"What on earth does he have against such creativity?" pondered Oscar, then answering his own question: "an envy of the womb, no doubt."

"But I didn't make you up!" she protested.

"Yes, you did! Can you not see that that is precisely what you did? First you made me up, and then you made me happen. I think your man Freud is as right as sunshine on a clear day. You are quite delusional."

"He hasn't said a word of this to me directly, of course. He never speaks these days," she added thoughtfully.

"Of course not. What need has he for speech? You are doing both sides of the analysis well enough without his help."

"You are humoring me, Oscar. But it's a terrible problem. His belief that I am delusional holds me back. Unless he thinks I am sane, he won't ever approve of my practicing psychoanalysis."

"That reveals a lack of vision, my dear. Does Freud think his future practitioners will all be sane? That's hardly likely, given the playing field he is playing on."

"Well, his other...what shall I call them? His other disciples seem a bit off to me, Jung in particular."

"Exactly. That is the way of it. Now. How angry are you at your dear Sigmund for not believing you about me?"

"What a question! I haven't a clue. I haven't asked that of myself, and I should have, of course." She took a deep breath. "Now that I focus on the matter, I find that I am in a frothing rage."

"Then we must act promptly. We can't let this man continue with his delusion about your delusion if it causes you discomfort. We must rip the pleasant fantasy he has constructed for himself right out from underneath him, like a magician removing a tablecloth at a dinner party."

"But how?" she puzzled.

"How?" He smiled, and waited.

"You're going to go see him! Oh, Oscar. It's too, too utterly, utterly perfect! You're going to the eminent Dr. Sigmund Freud not to be cured, but to cure him!"

"It is my fashion."

They talked until the wee hours of the afternoon when Oscar finally dozed and when he awoke Eleanora lay sleeping beside him. He watched her even breathing, noticed the health of her complexion and the happiness of her quiescent smile. In her man's suit and fresh linen, with hair bobbed into short dark curls that clung to her brow, she appeared to him very like the young men that he fancied. Looking closer she was, of course, womanly, with lines of age beginning to show at the edges of her eyes and mouth, the distressing feminine landscape of her figure beneath the tweeds.

Perhaps it was his stare that summoned her to consciousness. Eleanora's eyelids flickered, and she awakened with a full smile of satisfaction stolen from the realm of her dreams.

"I have always wanted to sleep with you, Oscar," she confessed.

Oscar smiled, and bestowed a gentle kiss on her brow. "You see? There is nothing to it," he replied.

CHAPTER 23

Note from Oscar Wilde

VENICE, ITALY
February, 1912

It was in that autumn of 1904 that Eleanora and I began the habit of sharing a bed together whenever I was in Vienna, most innocently, and mostly innocent.

CHAPTER 24

The Austrian poet, Rainer Marie Rilke, sat in the sculpture studio, happily watching the inexhaustible master at his work. Rodin was sculpting the head of a man. On many occasions Rilke had glimpsed this man, who sometimes stayed as a guest in the La Folie Neufbourg. The man—he believed his name to be Francis something or other—was a mystery about the house; there, but not there; never referred to, never seen openly except at a distance, for he sometimes walked in the gardens as dawn was breaking or night was falling. Was he, perhaps, an escaped criminal of some sort? Or a lunatic? He was never seen at Meudon where Rose Beuret kept a somewhat more legitimate household than here at La Folie. Could it be, Rilke wondered, that Aveline had taken a lover? I will never understand the French, thought Rilke, so untidy in their affairs. Perhaps he should simply ask Rodin who the man was. He hadn't the nerve, he realized. So he watched.

Auguste Rodin was aware of Rilke's curiosity. He worked away under the poet's gaze enjoyably. Let him wonder, he thought. Wonder is good for a poet. Oscar had sat for him formally only once. The rest of the image was formed from Auguste's close scrutiny of the man during their long talks, late at night, in the secret room. They were not precisely conversations. Wilde did most of the talking, Rodin listened and watched and rumbled a reply now and again. The man was a wizard with words.

Rodin would reveal Wilde's soul in this portrait. He would capture the intelligence, the humor, and the endurance. He would show the compassion. He would lay bare the suffering. And this time it would be seen. Other men in other places, men in museums, men in libraries, would gaze on this sculpture and want to know this man; would want to know who he was and how he lived and when he died.

Rilke was mesmerized. The hands of Rodin, at work upon his art, whether drawing or sculpting, thrilled the poet. He watched as the clay formed and reformed under the power of Rodin's powerful fingers, the prodding of his thumbs. Stroke and after stroke, in short bursts of glory, he brought forth his model from within his memory. There was something erotic in the event, and Rilke's body responded gently beneath his garments. His courage aroused, he asked at last: "Auguste, what is the name of this sculpture?"

"Head of a man," replied Rodin.

CHAPTER 25

Professor Dr. Sigmund Freud opened the door to his consulting room expecting his eleven o'clock patient as usual. He looked forward to his meetings with Lady Eleanora Ashburton. She was to Freud a fascinating case and a potential disciple, if he could cure her. To date her delusional system continued to elaborate, not dissipate, though her intellect had improved, and her appearance had undergone a remarkable change.

Instead of Lady Ashburton, Freud was surprised to find a large, middle-aged man sitting cross-legged on the plush red sofa. The man was smoking a cigarette and reading a leather bound volume of Shakespeare's plays.

"Who, may I ask, are you?" queried Freud.

The man looked up, blinked, recalled his present surroundings and smiled. Leaving the forests of Arden between the covers of his book, he stood up and, towering over Freud, extended his hand. "I am Oscar Fingal O'Flahertie Wills Wilde," he answered, "known for some years as Sebastian Melmoth, now taking the name of Francis Canterville. I am very pleased to meet you, Dr. Freud. I have heard much about you from our mutual acquaintance, Lady Eleanora Ashburton. She says you are a genius and sends her regards which is, of course, the same thing."

Intrigued, Freud stepped forward and took the proffered hand that all but swallowed his own. "She says you are a genius, too, Mr. Wilde."

"Well, that's settled then. We are both geniuses."

"Where, may I ask, is Lady Ashburton at the moment?" queried Freud.

"As we speak, she is having her hair dyed a more beguiling shade of strawberry blond. She sent me in her stead. There appears to be some misunderstanding between the two of you that she believes I can put right."

Freud bowed his head slightly and indicated the office door.

Oscar took his direction, and entered the enclave.

"Why this is charming," admired Oscar, looking about the room, "quite charming. It is full of beautiful things. Your office is nothing at all like my father's surgery. He was a medical man, too, you know, a specialist in eyes and ears. He was appointed the Surgeon Oculist to the Queen in Ireland, although our Dear Victoria visited that fair isle but once in her life and, alas, her eyes and ears did not require attention."

"I did not know this fact Mr. Wilde," said Freud. "There are published accounts of your father's life which fail to mention the Queen's eyesight. And I have read some accounts of your own life as well. You have been an object of interest to me for some time now. Sit there, opposite to me, while we talk." He gestured to a comfortable chair.

"Would you mind if I were to recline on your famous couch?" asked Oscar.

"As you wish," replied Freud without affect.

"Are you sure your neutrality is good for one? This studied acquiescence might drive a lesser mind mad."

"It is my method to evoke madness, Mr. Wilde, and then to cure it."

Oscar draped himself along the length of the couch in a languorous pose, but head to foot, in such as way as to converse with Freud face to face. The doctor took a cigar from a carved box near his own chair. Wilde lit a fresh cigarette produced from a silver cigarette case.

"You are kind to welcome me," said Oscar. "The world, including you, believes that Oscar Wilde, wit and playwright, is dead and buried. You must think me an impostor."

"Quite the contrary, Mr. Wilde," said Freud, between vigorous puffs on the recalcitrant cigar. "I knew instantly that you are whom you claim to be."

"You believe me?" It was Oscar's turn to be curious.

"Indeed."

"How do you come by your certainty? Lady Ashburton tells me that you are a man cautious in the extreme."

"Your physical size fits the descriptions I have read of you, and your chin is distinguishing; but a clever fraud would be chosen for his size and his chin. No, it was something you did quite unconsciously when first I addressed you in the waiting room. You leaned forward the better to hear me, but inclined, ever so slightly, to the left."

"So I must be compensating for the slight deafness in my right ear that resulted from the infection that led to my—how should I say it?—my supposed death. I was not even aware that I was favoring my good ear in this manner."

"An impersonator would not be so subtle."

"Well then, all the papers I have brought as proof that I am indeed the pudding, and all the arguments on my own behalf are rendered thoroughly unnecessary by your sharp powers of observation. Lady Eleanora's account of me is vindicated and her sanity, no doubt, proven?"

Freud nodded in assent. His cigar was going nicely now.

"May we converse then, for remainder of the hour? Repartee with a man of your intelligence would be a rare pleasure for me, and I am quite interested in your work. Lady Eleanora sends me your monographs as they are given to her. *Wit and Its Relation to the Unconscious* has beguiled me utterly."

"I am pleased to hear this, Mr. Wilde, for your work is in no small way its inspiration. I find the hostility that underlies your particular humor most interesting. You seem furiously angry with the conventions of society but seldom do you attack a specific individual."

"What would be the point? Most people are merely creatures of society. They do the best they can with the habits they have acquired. It is convention, the fountainhead of these deadly habits that must be undermined. Or so I once thought."

"We could converse about these and other matters, if you wish, and doubtless the pleasure would be mine, but you have expressed an interest in my work. Would you not learn more from an hour of serious psychoanalysis than from an equivalent time passed in amiable conversation?"

"I have never regretted my choice to live for pleasure, Dr. Freud."

"Let us move beyond the pleasure principle," Freud encouraged.

He looked deeply into Oscar's eyes, found his suffering, grasped it with his gaze, and held it unflinchingly.

"You are very compelling, Dr. Freud," replied Oscar. He turned himself around then, abandoning the pose of the aesthete, and lay down now in a more accepted manner on the couch. "How unusual it is to speak with someone I cannot see," he commented. "It is charming. Now I am to say whatever comes into my mind?"

Freud was silent. A patient who took his silence for affirmation revealed one kind of character to him; a patient who read disapproval from the silence, another.

"So much races through my brain—memories, fantasies, thoughts, fears."

Freud was silent. A man with too much to say revealed one kind of mind to him; a man with too little, another.

"I know!" declared Oscar. "I shall pretend that you are a passenger on a train seated next to me. You are blind. I am looking out the window at the passing scenery. I will tell you as much of what I see as I can manage. That will have to do. All right?"

Freud, who was phobic of trains, shifted uncomfortably in his chair, queasy at the thought; but he said nothing.

Wilde continued: "I remember a night in Paris. It was in the summer of 1900, and I was standing on the Pont des Arts wondering what the twentieth century would bring into being. That particular bridge is a pedestrian bridge that reaches out from the Louvre on the right bank to the Académie des Beaux-Arts on the left, very near the Hôtel d'Alsace where I lived during the last months of my decline. On the night of which I speak I was already gravely ill. I knew I had only a few months, maybe only weeks, to live. The doctors told me that if I were to cease drinking there was some hope, but I was addicted to absinthe at the time."

Prudence whispered to Oscar, cautioning him to reveal himself with more discretion. Oscar silently assured her it was safe to unburden himself to this man.

Freud noticed the slight hesitation, and thought to question it, but Patience, whom he knew better than Oscar, said: *be silent, wait.*

"I could not have ceased drinking, even if I had wanted to. However, I was quite sober on the night of which I speak, standing on the bridge, for I had no money left, and no credit to purchase drink. I was admiring the city with a clear vision. Paris lit from within is so incomparably beautiful, the dark shapes of the buildings, the occasional pleasure boat upon the river churning up a mélange of watery reflections. The moon was full. The air was cool. I lit a cigarette."

Freud noticed the silver cigarette case that Oscar fondled as he spoke. He recalled from reading the account of the trials how Oscar had chosen to give cigarette cases to his young male lovers. A little box of phallic objects waiting to be ignited. He recalled the scene of the missing cigarette case in *The Importance of Being Earnest.* A confession of Wilde's sexual preoccupations had been delivered, disguised as entertainment, on the London stage. Brilliant, he judged.

Oscar continued: "Down along the river's edge, on the footpath that runs along its bank, figures moved in perfect pools of golden lamplight. I knew there were beautiful boys among them, or boys made beautiful by the night, when in the shadows their soiled clothing becomes the raiment of royalty, and their skin is washed clean by moonlight. I stood for a long time, wondering if I should descend among them, but that night I did not do so. It was not because of the shortage of money, for I could beguile a boy with my talk and pay him later. It was the contentment that wrapped itself around me.

"I stood, in a state of grace, and I marveled that one so ruined as myself, one so outcast from the society that had once courted and coddled me, one so utterly despised and alone could feel myself filled up with love. I loved the blackness of the river and the night, the moon in contest with the dark, the outlines of museum walls enfolding the gifts of centuries past. I loved the boys below me in the lamplight and the heavens above me. All that I saw, all that I heard, I loved. Is that not astonishing, Dr. Freud? After what life had dealt me, I still loved life so much?"

Oscar paused, and removed another cigarette from his silver case. He lit the cigarette from the one before and inhaled deeply, then commented. "The cigarette, the cigar, they are the most perfect of civilized pleasures. Don't you agree, Dr. Freud? They give pleasure, but fail to satisfy."

Freud, wreathed in warm smoke, smiled from within the slightly altered state of consciousness into which he fell when listening to a patient.

"Now here is the thing," said Oscar, returning to his narrative. "In that perfect moment, that moment of stillness and peace, a thought occurred to me to leap from the bridge into the Seine. I thought, to die now, suffused with joy, before the miseries of life take hold again, why that would be an act of genius. The contradiction of feeling: the pure joy of life and the desire to have done with it, held me enthralled for several minutes. The coal-black water beckoned, the air embraced me. To which lover should I incline? And then the moment passed. My cigarette had gone out. I lit another. I turned from the spectacle of night and went back to my dingy room, to my debts, to my disgrace, and what I believed would be my natural demise. What do you make of it, Dr. Freud?"

There was a long silence. Oscar shifted on the couch and prepared to speak again. Patience counseled patience. *Don't you ever tire of your own advice?* Oscar asked her. *Not yet,* she replied.

Freud cleared his throat and spoke quietly. "On this night you relived an emotional experience from your childhood. Your mind was in the present reality but your emotions were of the past. You have spoken of your father to me. He came to mind as you observed the archaeological artifacts that adorn my office. As I told you, I have read of your father. Sir William Wilde was famous for four things: his medical specialty, his archaeological researches into Ireland's past, his promiscuity, and his unclean appearance. Consciously, you did not love your father, who had little time for his sons. Unconsciously, you longed for him, fascinated by his intellect and his dirt, by his love of life and the disgrace he brought upon your family."

It was Oscar who listened now.

"Your mother was famous for four things, also: her fiery, romantic poetry, her brilliant soirées filled with literary and political lights, her fierce loyalty to what and whom she loved, and her desire to remain beautiful. As a child you were pulled apart by these strong, contrasting personalities. Your emotions on the night you describe revisit your struggles. There below you are the dirty men, there above you, the brilliant stars of your mother's eyes. There below you, the blackness of your father's fingernails, there above, the warmth of mother's arms holding you tight. You long for both. You have longed all your life for a united family, a way to cherish both father and mother, men and women, sacred and profane, the old and the young."

He paused for effect. Oscar noted the theatrical touch, then as Freud's words washed through him, he began to experience a maddening combination of feeling: joy, at becoming known in this entirely new way; and sadness, at what was becoming known.

Freud continued: "When you stood on the stage in your aesthetic costume, your linen as immaculate as baby's lace, you were your mother's child. When you covered a guttersnipe with kisses, your father's. When as a scholar, at Portora, Trinity, and Oxford, you turned your mind toward ancient civilizations you were, unconsciously, in conversation with your father. When you charmed society's crème de la crème at a London dinner party, you fulfilled your mother's aspirations. And though it is your mother who inspired you to live, your father has called to you from the time he entered his Irish grave."

"And the moment of grace?" asked Oscar eagerly, "Before the idea to leap to my death assailed me?"

"Ah, this was from a yet earlier time, before the Oedipal battles began. The heat of the cigarette in your mouth, the pleasant air surrounding your body, the lap of nearby water—this combination of stimuli served as a powerful reminder of the warmth and nourishment you experienced when held to your mother's breast. You could see the boys across the expanse of the river. They represent both the boy you once were, longing to be loved by father, and father himself—alive, masculine and within your reach—but not near enough to intrude on the blissful communion with your mother."

"My mother," whispered Oscar, "Speranza. Hope."

"This has been a love and a loss of which you have been fully conscious. Love for, and from, your father was the unconscious hope."

"Do you think I will lose my desire for boys if I admit the need for a father's love? That would be so sad, as I have just recovered my desires."

"The sorrow is for your father's lost love. You are a bisexual man with brilliant gifts. You have been able to sublimate some of your internal conflicts and to act out the others with the young men you pursue. A paradoxical resolution, would you not agree?"

"It is true that I have thought of myself as both brilliant and paradoxical," Oscar concurred, "but I have never thought of myself as bisexual. The idea is too complex. I am a creature of the sixth inclination, and thereby, the simplest of lovers."

"The sixth inclination? I have heard of the English phrase, the sixth sense, but what is the sixth inclination? Please enlighten me, Mr. Wilde."

"There are men who are inclined to love women. That is the first. And its counterpart, women who are inclined to love men. That is the second. The third and fourth inclinations are obvious: men who love men, women who love women. The fifth inclination is what you would call your true bisexual, the lover of both men and women."

"And who is left, Mr. Wilde?"

"Those of the sixth inclination. Those men and women who, without stopping to make sexual distinctions at all, simply love those who are lovable."

"Is there not then a seventh inclination?" asked Freud after moment's pause.

"Now it is my turn to seek enlightenment. What would be the seventh inclination, Dr. Freud?"

"Those, of either gender, who, without stopping to make sexual distinctions, simply love those who are unlovable."

"You are thinking of Bosie Douglas."

"Yes."

"Many have found him unlovable, it is true. Many hold him responsible for my downfall, and so dislike him without knowing him. But when I first laid eyes upon him, he was, to me, perfection, and entirely made for loving."

"He represented, at last, the perfect combination of your love objects: his masculinity a reminder of your father, his beauty and breeding the idealization of your mother."

"Dr. Freud, does everything in my life reduce down to my attachment to only two people, to two love objects, as you so charmingly refer to them in your essays? My mother and my father? Others have held importance to me."

Freud was silent.

"There was my brother, Willie. A journalist. An embarrassment to me. During the time when I was on trial for my forbidden sexual practices he defended me as an honorable man. He told an acquaintance that I could be trusted with any woman in London." Oscar shook his head. "What a fool he was. Still, I loved him, in my fashion."

Freud again chose silence.

"And my dead sister, Isola Francesca. Abate Antonio, of whom you have heard through Lady Eleanora, once spoke of her and a stake of hot, white light ran through my heart as he said her name."

Freud put out his cigar, silently. He waited.

It was then that Oscar's eyes began to fill with tears. "And what of my two half-sisters, my father's natural daughters by another woman? I loved them so much. They were beautiful young women, loving and charming."

"And what became of these half-sisters, Mr. Wilde?" encouraged Freud, though he knew.

"They burned to death at a party. They were but sixteen and seventeen. Their fashionable clothing killed them. The full skirts of the elder girl swept unseen across the embers of a fireplace. Her petticoats went up like a torch; the younger died trying to put out the flames that engulfed her elder sister." He stopped to take a deep breath and then continued: "Later, when I wrote of women's fashion, I championed a free and natural form of dress, without bustles or petticoats—that Duncan woman, the dancer, has the idea. No one who read my articles knew why I wrote as I did, why I cared what women wore. Many found a man's interest in fashion distasteful. They had not seen petticoats aflame."

Oscar paused to wipe away his tears. "When Lady Eleanora told me about her brother Bertram and of how he died in that hideous gun accident, and how you have helped her face that which you term her survivor's guilt, I knew that I had a dose of the same disease. There are rumors that when I died in Paris it was of syphilis. But it was not of syphilis. It was of guilt. Guilt that I had lived on when all my pretty sisters died around me."

"That is only a partial explanation, Mr. Wilde, for it leaves out the essential point. It is true that you roared headlong toward your own destruction for many years. It is true that the engine of your self-destruction was unconscious survivor guilt. But, in so far as you died at all, you died of an ear infection, one you neglected, that in time entered into your brain. It was an ear infection that your father could have easily cured. Unbeknownst to your conscious mind, you were going to go to him in death, to take to him your troubles at last."

"When I was a man about town in London, I used to say that I lived in fear of being understood."

"By yourself or by others?" queried Freud.

"At the moment, by you, Dr. Freud. Tell me what else you make of my trials."

"Ah yes. The trials. There was yet another trauma in your childhood, Mr. Wilde. When you chose to repeat it, quite unconsciously, it ruined you."

"You leave no turn unstoned, Dr. Freud. I believe you refer to the infamous libel suit resulting from my father's promiscuity that took place in my youth."

"Libel suits are unusual things. To find a libel suit in two successive generations suggests a repetition compulsion is at work."

"I confess I do not know what drove me to press the libel charges against Bosie's father when he accused me publicly of sodomy. I blamed Bosie for goading me into the litigation, but if I am completely truthful with myself, I was compelled by some force within myself to prosecute the blackguard, and in so doing I brought disgrace on my own head. Is this the repetition compulsion of which you speak? Why would I want to repeat my boyhood humiliations?"

"When we repeat a trauma from our childhood, we are giving

ourselves another chance to face what hurt us so badly; we try to influence its outcome, to bring our adult powers to bear in a way we could not do as children. We unconsciously hope that the new version of the trauma will come out better for us in our present reality."

"Unconscious hope. It is a difficult concept, Dr. Freud. And it doesn't work, this repetition business. It came out badly again."

"Of course it came out badly. How could it not? We have to choose, Mr. Wilde. We have to choose to remember our traumas, face them, mourn them, and put them into our past; or else we will endlessly repeat them. Perhaps now you will choose a new path, one untrodden, as you have been awakened from the sleep of your past."

"'To die; to sleep: to sleep: perchance to dream…'"

"Shakespeare was ahead of me," Freud responded ruefully. "Well, our time is almost up, Mr. Wilde."

Oscar sat up, rubbing his eyes like a child. "A most unusual way to spend one's time, Dr. Freud. A unique experience. I feel as if I have been upended and dipped into the stream of the past. I have had a baptism by the Baptist himself!"

"You must be quite angry with me to make such a comparison, Mr. Wilde. You would have my head on a plate?"

"I resist this last interpretation, Dr. Freud. Why, were I to reside in Vienna, I would make a habit of calling upon you regularly. I hear you are 'at home' six days a week!"

"I think you will make a habit not to reside in Vienna," pronounced Freud. "Those who are drawn to psychoanalysis are also repulsed by it."

"Do you think I, like Lady Eleanora, would make a good psychoanalyst?"

"It is a charming idea," said Freud. He could not recall the last time he had used the word 'charming' in conversation. He stood up, indicating the doorway by which to leave the office.

Oscar stood up also, but, like many patients, he was unready to end the session. "You know, for the first time in many years, I feel eager to write again, to be putting black on white, black on white. I believe it is this curious psychoanalytic perspective on my life that has roused my muse from slumber. She had quite despaired of hearing anything new in the world. I believe you are a force for good, Dr. Freud. You have changed me in the course of this brief hour. Perhaps you and your teachings will change the world."

"Well, I have left your narcissism intact, but I believe it may be a healthy narcissism. Psychoanalysis will change the world for a time; whilst the ideas remain a novelty. Then it will disappear under the force of collective repression." Freud picked up a small statue from his desk, one that had been excavated in the valley between the Tigris and the Euphrates. He turned it over lovingly in his hands as he continued: "From time to time its truths will be rediscovered and then buried again."

"Rather like me," commented Oscar. "But why do you make this grim prediction for your science?"

"In your play, *An Ideal Husband,* you wrote: 'One's past is what one is.'"

"Yes, the line was quite well received."

"But, in truth, Mr. Wilde, no man wants to know that the child he once was still rules the adult he has become." Freud replaced the statue with a sigh. "Still, we hope to leave a mark, do we not, Mr. Wilde? To scratch 'Sigmund was here,' or 'Oscar was here' upon the rock face of history. We wish to contribute things of value to the consciousness of man. I wonder, in one hundred years will our names even be known? And if the names of Freud and Wilde are known, in what kind of mind will they be known?"

"And if they are unknown," Oscar countered, "by what kind of mind will they be unknown?"

"Ah. How you turn everything on its head and make it more interesting!"

"Inversion is one of my gifts."

Freud smiled. "I have enjoyed our work together, Mr. Wilde. I hope I have been of help to you."

"Indeed. I have learned a great deal, Dr. Freud. And I thank you for the hour."

"And what is it that you have learned from me, Mr. Wilde?" asked Freud, opening the door in a courtly, but decisive manner.

"I once said that any man can make history, but it takes a great man to write history."

"Yes? And now?"

"Were I to be given a forum, I would say: every man has a history, but it takes a great man to understand that history."

"You have a forum, Mr. Wilde. You have your writing."

"Good day, Dr. Freud."

"Good day, Mr. Wilde."

And the door of history was closed between the two men of genius.

CHAPTER 26

The Memoirs of Aveline Tartine

LA FOLIE NEUFBOURG, PARIS

Oh, my Dear Uncle Oscar. How you would laugh to know that you are the darling of the current age, and Freud is in disrepute!

These chapters of the memoir of Oscar Wilde, which he wrote in the third person and entitled, rather cleverly I believe, *The Return of the Century,* came to me as did all the rest—anonymously. I first read them with eagerness as I thought they might give me a clue as to his final disappearance from our lives. Indeed they did, but it was only when my mysterious correspondent was about to give up his ghost that I learned for certain what had happened to Oscar, as you will in due time.

In the meantime, it is necessary to share the comings and goings at La Folie Neufbourg for the sake of Posterity, whom I imagine is a distant and not very bright niece of Patience.

Once I adored being at the center of such artistic life.

But after ten decades…one tires. I would rather be eating chocolates. Nevertheless, here is a letter from George Bernard Shaw to the actress Ellen Terry, with whom he shared only an epistolary romance. How dull!

Paris
April, 1906

My Dearest Ellen Terry, the wan lily of my life…

As you know, I now sit patiently before the master, Auguste Rodin. Rilke says that I pose with the same vital sincerity with which I write. Could mere sitting be vital? Sincere? Yes. When one sits for Rodin it is so! You imagine in your letter to me that I will have lovely, peaceful times during the sittings. There you go astray. Yesterday he had me sit in a child's seat. Can you imagine how this worked on my mind? I felt young and old, solemn and playful, serious and ridiculous all at once. Then—and I must say, this amused me greatly—he decapitated the sculpture on which he had been working and with much ferocity! I sit at about an arm's length from Auguste, and in that moment I would have been happier a wee bit further back.

In truth, I believe the portrait-bust will be a fine thing—though not, as you suggest, like Pan—and I am glad I came to Paris, although it is, of course, Paris.

Now for the best part. You won't believe whom Auguste Rodin has sealed up in his closet. I will tell you, if you first write to me with all your guesses, and if, by the time I receive them, I don't think the whole thing was only a bizarre dream.

George Bernard Shaw

P.S. Rodin is peeved with Rilke for his hero-worshiping attitude towards me! Would it not be a fine thing if great men could have feelings somewhat above the average?

CHAPTER 27

O scar was all aglow with the news he had just received. Wishing to
bask in his happy anticipation, he hired a gondola and allowed
himself to be taken across the lagoon; a journey that took fully half the
morning. A morning well spent. Languor, he reflected, is not appreciated by half.

But by the time he reached the Isola Francesco del Deserto he was
eager to share his letter with Abate Antonio and he jumped onto the
little pier with the nimbleness of a youth, leaving the gondola to seesaw
merrily in the shallow water.

Oscar made his way hastily up the carefully tended gravel path and
rang the bell for entry. Fra Ricardo peered at him through the peephole
in the thick, wooden door and, as quickly as it was possible, opened
the portal. The two men embraced each other, bestowing symmetrical
kisses on alternate cheeks in the Italian style. Two long years had passed
since they had last seen one another. For Oscar they had been important
years, largely spent in solitude, as he lay down the outline of his memoir,
and began to glimpse the shape of his future.

"Is it Oscar Wilde or Sebastian Melmoth or Francis Canterville these
days?" asked the smiling friar. "Or have you taken yet another nom de
plume?"

"One can never have enough Christian names, can one, Fra Ricardo?"

"And you are in good health I see, but perhaps need a strong tea
nevertheless. What shall it be? Chamomile? St. John's Wort? Vanilla,
I think, for celebration. Come along now to the Cloister of Swallows.

Your feathered friends sigh between songs, for they miss you greatly. I will tell Abate Antonio that you are here."

Oscar had never heard so many words tumble from the lips of his reticent friend.

"You have kept up with your English, Fra Ricardo."

"God speaks in every tongue. Though I wish His English spellings were more consistent."

"Ah, yes. *I* before *E*, except when it isn't."

Oscar was surprised at how small the cloister actually was. In his memory it had grown to twice the size. The birds fluttered and twittered and lit upon his shoulder one by one. Some he recognized. Most were the children and grandchildren of the birds he had known, all of them bold and interested in making a friend of him. The old peacock strolled about pretending not to notice the visitor, his beak out of joint, but keeping a sharp eye on him.

"Don't be so aloof," chided Oscar. "I have brought you your favorite sweetmeat." And he drew from his pocket a slice of almond cake, bought in haste from a café on the Fondamenta Nove for this particular bird. The peacock was quick to accept the cake from Oscar and to fan his feathers in response.

"So you do not forget your old friends," said Oscar with satisfaction.

It was then that the Abate came upon them, Hector perched proudly on his shoulder. "And you do not forget yours!" said the abbot.

"Abate Antonio! How good to see you. You look a little pale. And Hector!"

"He, at least, has all his color."

"I have brought you both a treat." Oscar handed the parrot an almond dipped in chocolate.

"Greed!" squawked Hector and reached for the offering.

"And for me?" asked the Abate, holding out his hand in claw-like imitation of the bird.

"Look at this letter, my friend!" He placed the paper in the abbot's hand, but went on to disclose its contents before there was time to read it. "Claude Monet has agreed to visit Venice at last. I have cajoled and prodded for years. The place was made for him. And it so needs a touching up. I know you love his work, far more than I, though he has won me over to Impressionism, brushstroke by brushstroke, in these last few years. I shall host a small dinner party for us in my rooms, and you can show him the beauties of Venice."

"These are good tidings indeed," exclaimed the Abate. "Is he not too old to make the journey in comfort?"

"He shall have for his troubles the October light upon the Ducal Palace! Oh, he will capture the spirit of the place for the first time since Turner!"

"It is wonderful to see you so full of spirit, my friend, and is it only to be the messenger of this fine news that you trouble yourself to cross the waters? Do you not take your Gypsy woman's warnings with any seriousness? Fear death by water."

"You chide me for my strange enthusiasms. I take a fortuneteller's advice only if I happen to agree with it. But I do have a question for you, Abate, and it is about the future. It is a question that troubles my spirit and you may be able to help me."

"Come into your old room. We have kept it as you left it, in case you returned to us, or another resurrected poet was in need of a bed."

Soon they were seated before a fire that Fra Ricardo had coaxed to a happy blaze. Hector sat happily on his old perch, waiting for the toasting of bread to begin. Here in the cell, with a good brandy in hand, Oscar found he was reluctant to talk.

"It is so peaceful here, Abate. I am loathe to stir the air with troubles."

"Then tell me of your writing. Lady Ashburton wrote me at Yuletide last that you were at work on a novel. It must be well along by now."

"Yes. It is really a memoir, but as memoirs never sell, I call it a novel. It is entitled *The Return of the Century,* and you are in it, of course, even as we speak. That old charlatan Freud has quite unblocked my creative powers."

"You need not call him a charlatan on my behalf, Oscar. He is clearly a force to be reckoned with in this new century. Now that I have read more of him, I find his ideas provocative, but valuable. Alas, he knows nothing of God."

"But God knows of Dr. Freud. He was at His most wonderfully

creative when he thought up Sigmund. My own work goes well also."

"When can I read it?" asked the Abate with evident enthusiasm.

"Oh, it's in a terrible pile of pieces at the moment. I work on it whenever I come to Venice. Venice seems to be my precondition for writing. So far it is but a few loose chapters, a few notes, musings. I am trying to make something of all the things that I have undergone, and all things my friends have undergone in the interests of keeping me undergoing."

"And do you write with humor?"

"Freud would say so. Of course the light and witty Oscar died on the way to prison. So what voice now?"

"The poet?"

"Gone the way of all things."

"The critic?"

"Likewise. I have had to create myself anew. I've been trying out the voice of a wise man, a sage, a seer. I've stolen it in part from you."

"Theft!" squawked Hector.

"Perhaps you should steal from yourself," said the abbot.

"Oh, I used to do that all the time, and I was always being criticized for it."

"But surely you have enough experience now to be wise." The abbot quoted Wilde to himself:

"Being ourselves the sowers and the seeds,
The night that covers and the lights that fade,
The spear that pierces and the side that bleeds,
The lips betraying and the life betrayed."

"I was a youth when I wrote that. One would imagine that given these extra years I would have learned so much more, perhaps the very meaning of life."

"You've lived these last years as a good man, Oscar."

"To be good is easy. It requires merely a certain amount of sordid terror, a certain lack of imaginative thought, and a certain low passion for middle-class respectability."

"But you have been kind to others. Surely that has been wise."

"I have been kind to those I care about. A small kind of kind. Less than kind."

"There is a reason why people reach for God in all his magnificence, Oscar. The world and its ways are too small without Him."

"Is it really, Abate? Do we need a heaven full of angels, when the sky is filled with birds?"

"You know how to argue with a Franciscan."

"I know how to argue with anyone. It is a gift. You know when I went to Rome after my release from Reading Goal, I was blessed three times by the His Holiness. The blessings grew and became these unexpected years upon the earth. I see all this, Abate, but still I do not reach for God."

"Perhaps He already has you in the palm of his hand."

Oscar looked down, examining his own palm, his own unique, unrepeatable palm.

"When we are about to weep our voice breaks," said the abbot gently, "now you write, dear Oscar, with your broken voice."

The silence of the Isola lay between them for a while. Then the slap, slap of sandals was heard in the corridor. "Ah, here is Fra Ricardo again, this time with one of his herbaceous brews. Why not read to us some of what you have written. Let us feel the effect of it."

The three men settled themselves in the scent of vanilla tea. "I have the very beginning with me. It's a rough draft of course. But I shall read it out. Just the very beginning. I shall." Oscar removed the manuscript from his rucksack and began to read in his most mellifluous voice:

The Return of the Century
by Oscar Fingal O'Flahertie Wills Sebastian Melmoth
Francis Canterville Wilde.

It is said that dead men tell no tales. However, I have always found it charming to make of myself an exception to the rule.

Society believes that I am dead, but it is society that has died. I am merely older than anticipated, and younger than I feel, for, even the efforts of the miraculous friars on the Isola Francesco del Deserto could not restore me to the man I was before the prison years.

I will tell my story as a novel that will allow me to be omniscient, both sexes, and—when the manuscript is published—immortal. Again.

Though I am soon off to new adventures in America, I shall consign this document to a crevasse behind the loose stone of the wall, here, in the depths of this damp Venetian palazzo; a hiding place I discovered during the long hours of my solitude. I shall wrap the pages in waxed paper and seal them in a strong tin box. They will survive until my return. Should, however, I fail to return to Venice the manuscript will endure until discovered, decades from now, perhaps centuries from now. Or perhaps God will sink the entire palazzo beneath the waters of the Canal Grande, with only a ripple to mark its passing. Did not the sibyl tell me: "fear death by water"?

Darkness is creeping over Europe. War crouches in the shadows of time. Alas, events might prevent a homecoming. So I sit in the garden of the palazzo and imagine who you might be—my discoverer, my reader, my modern audience; you are lurking there in the tenebrous future where I cannot see you, somewhere after the battles are done…

Perhaps you are a German boy. Almost a man, beautiful and fair with a resemblance to your aged grandfather who has lost an eye to Prussia's prevailing dream. Your parents have occupied this watery city for a decade now. These beautiful Northern Italians, once the sovereigns of civilization, have become servants in their own demolished homeland. Oh, the art you Teutonics have destroyed! And now you, boy, alone at your baleful games, have found my manuscript in its tomb of stone.

Or, perhaps you are an American youth. A student, enterprising and sturdy, busily self-making yourself into manhood, heedless of your grandfather who fought and died to insure the freedoms you now take for granted; the freedom to stand at the window of this ancient abode listening to the gondolier below singing opera so badly.

How exotic it is to write to you; you, who are so unknown to me. But I have a wish that you will think of me. I have a wish to leave a certain impression. Think of me as I am now, poised with one foot at the grave of the past, and the other at the grave of the future. Here is my story. Remember me.

PARIS, FRANCE
November, 1900

The marble mantel clock stops its ticking at the moment of Oscar Wilde's last breath, and in the silence that follows one can hear the sound of unwritten books snapping shut forever...

Oscar stopped reading and his audience clapped appreciatively. "Delightful, Oscar," said the abbot, "and you see it was not forever. But why, may I ask, are you going to America? You once wrote that when good Americans die they go to Paris and when bad Americans die they go to America."

"Did I? How clever of me." He put the papers back in his pouch. "But now that I have performed for you, I will ask the question on which I need your advice."

The abbot nodded at Fra Ricardo who silently padded away. "Proceed."

"The news has come to me that I am to be disinterred. Now that Robbie Ross has paid off my debts—did you know he has managed to get my complete works published? They had a formal dinner to celebrate! Well, now that the body of my work is salvaged, my body itself is to be removed from Bagneux Cemetery to Père Lachaise Cemetery and given a proper monument."

"This was anticipated, was it not? By Rodin? When he made his likeness of you to fit the coffin? Still, it must be disconcerting."

"Indeed."

"What troubles you Oscar? Surely a better address is still of interest to you. Even among the society of the dead."

"My younger son, Vyvyan, and my friend, Robert Ross, are to be in attendance at the grave."

"I see."

"It will be a terrible temptation for me, with Vyvyan in Paris, and my knowledge that he is there, not to go to him, although I know this would be terribly unkind, after so much care has been taken to let him get on with a life without me. I once said, I can resist everything except temptation. I was simply telling the truth."

"And your son, Cyril?"

"He is not to accompany them. He's often abroad. Cyril makes a habit of adventurous exploits to prove his manhood. He must protest too much because of me."

"What would you want from a meeting with Vyvyan?"

"I simply want to see him."

"To what end?"

"To see him would be an end in itself."

"Then go. I have never been a supporter of this ruse, as you know."

"I sense it would hurt him. And I once told you that had I known my actions would cause harm to others, then I could not forgive myself."

"Then do not go as yourself."

"But to see him and not cry out—"

"You have a way to cry out, Oscar. Cry out in your work. Write of it. Write one of your beautiful prose poems. Someday, perhaps, that cry will be heard, and those who hear it will be moved to compassion."

"You have helped me, Abate."

"I only return a favor, Oscar."

"Whatever do you mean? How could I have been of help to you? I have brought naught but disturbance to the peace of this island."

"Those of us who are chosen for God's work leave the temptations of the flesh unanswered. Still, we are curious. And our own bodies betray us sometimes, in sleep, in reverie, always asking for some other."

"Lust!" shouted Hector.

"You have spoken of your life without censorship or remorse. Thereby, you raised doubt in my mind. I asked myself if I had missed out on life, here, on this lonely island. Surrounded by celibate men as remote as I from sensual passion. Do you know what I learned from the consideration of my doubts, Oscar? The doubts you inspired?"

"I cannot presume to guess."

"I learned the very meaning of life. And I shall tell you what it is. I learned—" But Abate Antonio did not finish his sentence. He looked quizzically at Oscar, then slumped heavily to the side. The Franciscan was caught by the wing of the chair, which kept him from falling, like a dead sparrow, onto the stone floor.

CHAPTER 28

The Grave Digger with Large Hands
A Prose Poem by Oscar Wilde

The gravedigger with large hands went about his work that summer day though he knew not happiness. Today he labored not to put a man into the earth as was the custom, but to bring forth a man who had lain there for nine long years. The damp French clay was heavy on his spade.

A gravedigger with dirty fingernails worked at his side, breathing hard, digging to find the coffin. The gravedigger with large hands liked not the man who worked beside him. He liked not the day, which was hot and humid and full of portent. He liked not the work, for it was to him a paradox and bode no good. So, he knew not happiness.

An undertaker, an undertaker's assistant, and two mourners came nigh to the place where labored the gravedigger with large hands. From his place, chest deep in the earth, the gravedigger with large hands did not at first see the men approach. When he did, his breath held. His spade paused momentarily in the hot and humid air.

One of the mourners was of middle-age and seemed to be in charge of the proceedings. This is the dead man's loyal friend, thought the gravedigger with large hands.

The second mourner was a younger man, slight, and delicate of feature. This is the dead man's son, thought the gravedigger with large hands.

The spade of the gravedigger with the large hands struck the lid of the coffin, and the difficult task of prying and lifting was soon underway. He felt that he might perish from the efforts of this day, and he knew not happiness.

A new casket was brought to the side of the grave. The gravedigger with large hands looked on as the old casket was opened and the mourners looked upon the man who had lain in the earth for nine long years. The mourners wept silently and with great dignity for they knew not happiness.

Soon the new casket held the heaviness of the dead man who had lain in the earth for nine long years, and it was about to be borne away when there appeared a problem with the new casket. The name on its cover read Oscard Wilde, the D, mistaken. The friend of the dead man was much disturbed when he saw the mistaken D, and angrily he railed at the undertaker. The son of the dead man was stoic. He is like a young prince, thought the gravedigger with large hands, and happiness came to him.

The undertaker took from the belt of the gravedigger with large hands a chisel and a heavy hammer, and he struck off the offending letter. It fell into the empty grave and the gravedigger with large hands picked it up. It was made of good brass. The D is for death, he thought. Death has been struck from this coffin. He gave the D that was made of brass to the gravedigger with dirty fingernails who smiled and went away for happiness had come to him.

Then the friend of the dead man and the son of the dead man went away with the coffin and with them went the happiness of the gravedigger with large hands. He was sad, for he could look no more upon the stoic young man who was like a prince, for he loved the young man as a man loves a son.

When night fell the gravedigger with large hands could still be found sitting in the bottom of the empty grave. He thought only of the stoic young man who was like a prince. And, from his place in this grave, he was looking at the stars.

Note from Oscar Wilde

I tried to write of the experience of seeing my son, Vyvyan, as part of my memoir, but, as the Abate suggested, it required a poem in prose. I have not yet seen Cyril, though I hear he may go to America on one of his adventures. I hope, perhaps, to see him there.

The monument that was placed on my new grave in Père Lachaise Cemetery is kept covered with a tarpaulin. Jacob Epstein, the sculptor, has been asked to add a pair of brass bathing trousers to the torso of the naked angel. He refuses.

CHAPTER 29

"Tell me what happened then," demanded Eleanora. "Abate Antonio always appeared healthy as a well-kept racehorse to me."

"He lies quietly since the stroke, but he does not speak. Perhaps he prays silently. He looked at me, for the few moments I was allowed to see him, with a mixture of compassion and irony. I've never seen anything quite like it before."

"So we are never to know the meaning of life?"

"It was *his* meaning, Eleanora. Not ours."

"I suppose so," she grumbled. "More champagne? Oh, dear. Your feet are still damp from the thunderstorm. Let me dry them for you." She knelt down and began to remove Oscar's shoes.

"Lady, on your knees to me? Get up you great fool."

They laughed and Oscar finished removing his shoes, drying his feet, drinking his champagne. "How I do love you, Eleanora. It seems that I lose everyone I love to death or distance. Are you not frightened for your life?"

"Oh, I shall live forever. Fate has no interest in the likes of me. Perhaps she only strikes us dead or dumb when we have discovered the meaning of life, which makes us both quite safe." Oscar could see her face, radiant with health and confidence as she spoke. She had indeed found herself. She was enjoying her life. Even her love for Oscar no longer hurt her, only warmed her. And yet a shudder went through him at her remark. Rain beat against the windows.

"Oscar, what's wrong? You've gone quite pale. I fear the damp has given you a chill."

"I'm quite all right," he reassured her. "It's only that I sense something coming. Sometime wicked in the times ahead of us. War, I think. And Vienna…" He shook his head. "Vienna will not be safe."

"Whatever are you on about, Oscar? Vienna has never been more gay."

"It's a feeling, Eleanora. A premonition. Something dark approaches us from without." As if to underscore his words, an enormous clap of thunder startled them into momentary silence.

"You shall have to go back to Dr. Freud, my dear. You are in the grip of a painful neurotic fantasy, probably precipitated by the abbot's stroke, or the horror of attending your own exhumation. Now *that* was a ghastly idea."

"I saw Vyvyan. He's a man now. A man to make me proud. I had to go. I owed it to Abate Antonio. He asked me to write about the experience, and I have done. Now, having gone to my own grave, so to speak, I need to spend a few weeks with you. I need to drink chocolate and be warmed by the light of you."

"And by my boys?"

"Well, you do have excellent taste in household help."

CHAPTER 30

The Memoirs of Aveline Tartine

Oscar when he came to La Folie, always came unannounced. It was on a clear autumn morning in 1908 when the hazelnut tree was golden-brown that he brought me the gift that would change my life. I remember that I was reading. I was midway through the last act of his most satisfying play *The Importance of Being Earnest* when he arrived carrying an unfamiliar leather valise. He had not stopped to greet Auguste, but had come straight to me in the blue sitting room. His face was aglow with the exertions of rapid travel and the delight in seeing me, but I discerned immediately that there would be no time for greetings. Something important was on his mind. Yes?

"Aveline," was all he said, clutching his bag awkwardly to his chest.

"My dear Uncle Oscar, what it is?" I asked in mild alarm.

"It's a boy, my squirrel, it's another boy."

"You are in love again!" I said, my concern changing swiftly to happiness, for I loved love. "How delightful! What is his name? How did you meet him? You don't suppose he will run off with Timothy Tyharde like the last one did!"

"I don't know his name yet. I met him, oddly enough, in a railway station," he answered. "But although I am smitten, it is not at all what you think. Look here." With that he carefully put the leather bag down on the tea table and opened it up. I hurried to see what was inside. It was a sleeping baby, swaddled in red flannel. The infant appeared to be newborn and in rosy good health.

At the sight of the baby, my heart leapt into the satchel and began beating in time with the infant's sleeping heart. No one could have been more surprised than me, for I thought of myself as without maternal calling. "Is it a foundling?" I asked.

"More or less."

"Could I have looked like this once?" I asked the question more to myself than to Oscar.

"More or less."

"Whatever are we to do with it?"

"More and more has been my experience."

"But how are we to feed it? You must tell me everything. Everything." I picked up the leather bag with extreme care and gently carried it to the sofa. Sitting down, I transferred the satchel to my lap, hoping the warmth of my body would make its way through the leather and blankets to the baby.

"I'll answer all your questions in good time, but I've learned to attend to my own needs whilst he sleeps. May I ring for tea and sweets? And I must have a moment to catch my breath and to let my thoughts catch me up."

I nodded, barely paying him any mind, and Oscar rang for Madeleine. He then dropped his overcoat onto the nearest chair and sat down next to me on the sofa. I had the impression that he wanted to be close to the infant. When the tea and cakes arrived we shut the handbag over the sleeping infant to shield him from Madeleine's prying eyes. Alone with each other again we re-opened the bag, and Oscar told me of his adventure.

"You know that I have been in Vienna? With Lady Eleanora Ashburton?"

"Yes. You have often gone to her over the years, and once she was here to visit you. But that was four or five years ago, yes? She wore a beautiful ensemble, and fine jewels. She was in love with Auguste, and with you, and was respectful of me. A good combination in a woman. I liked her."

"Eleanora had a propensity for falling in love with other women's men. And other men's men, for that matter, but when I went to her some time ago—when I was fleeing from Bosie in my petticoats, as you may recall—she was utterly changed in appearance. No more beautiful gowns, Aveline. No gowns at all. She wore a man's suit and tie."

"I did not think she was...how do the English say it? A lesbian woman."

"The English do not say it. Queen Victoria placed women who love women in the same category as elves and hobgoblins. They do not exist in the British Empire, and as the sun never sets upon same, they do not exist at all. But to answer your question, no, she had not become a lesbian. She was in love with me, as ever she was, and with Sigmund Freud—"

"Freud again! Doubtless, I will not understand."

"This time you will," Oscar assured me. "As I was saying, she was still in love with all kinds of hopeless situations in the form of unusual men, but she was very happy. She loved this new science, psychoanalysis, and declared that it had liberated her from all she found oppressive in English society."

"This I think is not such a bad thing."

"No, no, but it has had terrible consequences." He looked meaningfully into the satchel at the peacefully sleeping baby.

"This consequence cannot be thought terrible," I objected, already fiercely protective of the infant. "Even if this baby is Lady Ashburton's baby, which I think now it is, and without the husband, no?"

Oscar's face changed then. He grew pale. He looked quite stricken. He took Aveline's hand. "Aveline, my friend, the baby is Eleanora's, and its birth has cost her...her life."

We gripped one another's hands tightly over the sleeping infant. "Oh, Oscar, Dear Uncle Oscar. I am so sorry. I know that you loved her as the good, kind friend she was. How sad you must be."

"I have seldom been sadder," he concurred. "But unlike other times and other losses, I have been too busy to acknowledge my grief. The baby was, quite literally, thrust upon me. I was in the railway station in Vienna, stunned from the loss of Eleanora and eager to leave the city following her death. Her body was to be returned to England for burial. I thought, in so far as I could think at all, to go to Venice, or to the Isola, and mourn there in solitude. Suddenly a young man accosted me. He was very handsome, and I recognized him as one of Eleanora's minions, one of the youths she kept about the place to serve her. He was carrying a bundle wrapped in a red blanket. I knew instantly that he was carrying the baby, and I thought he must be, in fact, the father. He pushed the sleeping infant into my arms, and said, 'It's yours, Mr. Wilde, it's yours.'"

"Surely he didn't think—"

"I don't know what he thought. The young man turned and ran, literally ran, across the station and away. And I have run to you. I know I must protect this child. It is Eleanora's baby, after all. It is the very least I can do—its life in return for mine."

"How have you cared for it, all the way from Vienna? Surely it has not slept across three countries."

"A bottle full of milk was wrapped into the blanket, and the train people replenished it as needed. For nappies, I am afraid it has been wearing a half a dozen of my best handkerchiefs. He doesn't cry much when he wakens, or drool much either, which is a blessing as I cannot abide drooling."

"You'll become accustomed to it, I expect."

"I think not, Aveline. I was a poor father when my sons were in the nursery. I only wanted to see them clean, in good health, and fashionably dressed. More to the point, I think he must stay here at La Folie with you and Auguste and the servants all about. I can offer him no such accommodations. He cannot grow up in secret. When he does cry he makes entirely too much noise to be considered for a hidden life."

"You mean you want me to raise him up?"

"Who better than a foundling to raise a foundling? You must know everything not to do from your own experience. Auguste, as we all know, is a terrible father, but perhaps with both Oscar and Auguste two bad fathers will amount to one that is at least adequate."

"I think the fathers are not so important until he is five or six. No?"

"You see, Aveline, you understand Freud perfectly!" declared Oscar.

"Now I don't know what you are talking about! Look. He is stirring." Indeed the baby had begun to make tiny movements with his hands and mouth. I tenderly lifted him from the handbag, revealing the bottle of milk, quite warm, which had been tucked in alongside the infant. Tentatively I offered the milk to the baby, who took it readily.

"There. He likes you every bit as much as me, Aveline," said Oscar with both relief and sadness in his voice.

"Look at us, sitting here before the hearth, Dear Uncle Oscar. We look like a married couple; the husband somewhat older than the wife, sitting cozily with their new baby. What a long and strange way we have each traveled to find ourselves in such a homely moment."

The boy was called Alfred Earnest. Oscar would have it so.

I added Oscar Auguste to the parade of names, and his last name was given as Ashburton-Canterville. He was the greatest joy of my life. The baby and I were parted but once when Oscar insisted on taking him off to Venice; some urgent need of his to show off the boy to a fortuneteller. Alfred Earnest returned from Venice with his head full of gypsies and gondolas, and grew uneventfully to manhood here at La Folie.

Auguste was as bad a father to Alfred Earnest as he was to his own son, but he played his role as the illegitimate father (for the sake of propriety, said Oscar) to those who knew of the boy's existence for he thought it complimented his manhood. Vuillard, who became friendly with the youngster, helped out, especially after Oscar disappeared in 1912. He painted the boy several times.

Auguste and I produced no children of our own. So my relations, though all are acquired, have given me much satisfaction in life, particularly as they reside, for the most part, in England. Indeed I have outlived Alfred and his son, but my great grandson lives in London and visits when he can. He tries to talk me into living with him and his wife and two children, but I could not abide the English damp and the dampness of spirit that accompanies their weather. And to live with great great grandchildren. It would make me feel old. No? I will live out my days, and it is probably only a matter of days now, here where I have been happy, with the granddaughter of Madeleine as my only companion. It is as it should be. Madeleine was but a maid, though her daughter was by Auguste, the old ram.

Was Oscar the father of Alfred Earnest? Had Lady Eleanora Ashburton's love for Oscar at last been consummated? I like to think so. Yes. I saw much of Oscar in the boy, much kindness, much wit. But what mother doesn't see what she wishes in her child? There on that shelf is the handbag in which he arrived, next to the basket in which I arrived. Life is a strange business, no?

Now, you wonder, what happened to Timothy and Charles perhaps, yes? Or have you forgotten them? You young people are far too careless for my taste. We must…how do the Americans say it? Tie up all the loose behinds?

⤳

DRUMWILLIG, SCOTLAND

January, 1911

Dear Oscar (it is safe to call you Oscar on the inside of the letter, I presume)…

I am so sorry to hear that you will not be able to visit us in Drumwillig before your departure for America. Charles and I had so looked forward to showing you our home. It is utterly changed from the humble vicarage in which I was raised. Everything is beautiful: William Morris, Chippendale, and a series of Aubrey Beardsley drawings that are breathtaking. (I know you are lukewarm on Beardsley, but even you would admire these, I'm sure.)

Of course, the villagers are busy not knowing what they know and being kind and remote which is the best they can manage for the queer son of the cold, old vicar, now gone deep into the Scottish sod from which he sprang. Even a wee place like Drumwillig has its Society, and Charles and I are decidedly not to play a part within it. My worst fear is that they will relent and accept us! So far, we live here undisturbed by the slings and arrows of outrageous drinks parties.

I have been reading my way through Dickens (your assessment of Dickens is too severe, I think) and I go into the shop in Edinburgh on most days. The journey is only an hour, and the countryside, if one looks up, not down, as you have taught me to do, is charming. All of Edinburgh may seem antique to you, as you say, but within it are especial treasures to be found and polished up and carried off by the sharp-eyed tourists. You and our dear departed Eleanora were, of course, right about everything concerning my happiness.

Charles seems content as well. I keep a wary eye on him, for he may yet prove a bolter, but I don't think so. His Highland Suite in F minor is progressing well, and, of course with the table he sets for me each evening, my wiry beanpole figure is taking on the proportions of a self-satisfied country squire.

I hope that Aveline will allow little Alfred to come visit us in a year or two. He would love roaming about the countryside scaring the wildlife (or perhaps the wildlife scaring him, for he sounds a proper city boy to me!). We would be happy for his company, and the remembrance of Eleanora he would bring with him. His picture is the likeness of her. And he looks rather like you, too. (Do I imagine this?)

Perhaps you will accompany him here yourself, if America proves less welcoming than you imagine? Yes, I know you had a great success touring the United States in your youth: the audiences loved your speeches, the miners liked the way you drank whiskey, and Jefferson Davis talked to you in his garden about the glories of rebellion, while you admired his ability to fail in life on such a grand scale. But this time, dear Oscar, you will be just Oscar…or rather, Francis. Unknown in a country that admires only fame and success.

I agree that it was wicked of San Francisco to burn down. I know it was your favorite American city. But I question your second choice. Why Wyoming, one may be forgiven for asking?

Perhaps my retreat to the bucolic has influenced you unduly? Do rethink the idea of establishing a theatre in this most paradoxical of places. You are a city man, just as little Alfred is a city boy.

You will languish for lack of noise, loss of bother. Peace will be a plague to you, mark my word, particularly with buffalo roaming all over it. If these ancient vicarage walls will stand one more prayer within them, then I will pray that you reconsider your venture and be content simply writing and publishing again from a nice suite of rooms, with perhaps Chinese furniture (?) overlooking Washington Square Park in New York City, within a stroll of Delmonico's. But don't let an old Scottish stick deter you! Of course the idea of The Wyoming Shakespeare Company is charming. Will you produce only Shakespeare? Will you not be tempted to have a go at Shaw? Or even, dare I say it, Wilde, now that he is being performed again, even here in Britain?

Write to me immediately when you arrive in America and tell me of the journey, and of life as you find it in the Wild Wild West.

Or better still, write me from the ship. Pitch the note overboard in a bottle, addressed to me in Drumwillig. Fate will bring it to me, I am sure, for I will be waiting with Patience. I want to know every detail of the voyage as it occurs, and the nightlife—in every class—aboard the *R.M.S. Titanic*.

With a fond farewell, and bon voyage,

Timothy Tyharde

Now I have gotten your attention, yes? Fear death by water, said the gypsy.

This letter I received a week ago. It finally answered the question of Oscar's sudden disappearance from our lives. My friend, Anonymous, had decided to make himself known to me at last. Now you will know all that Aveline Tartine knows.

I will ring for the young Madeleine and we will have some champagne, and a strawberry cake. Let us drink to the future. Yes?

LONDON, ENGLAND

September, 1983

Dear Aveline Tartine...

I write to you now to reveal my identity. The doctor says it is now or never. My future is all behind me now. A future I would never have had at all were it not for the object of your affection and the mentor (perhaps father?) of your child, Alfred Earnest.

I write with honor and affection about Oscar Fingal O'Flahertie Wills Wilde.

I felt the letters, the manuscript, all the papers belonged within the family and have collected them and sent them along over the years as I felt they were safest in your keeping, though it has been hard to part with them. Oscar Wilde has held a special place in my heart for it was he who once saved my life. I was only eight years old and on board the *R.M.S. Titanic.*

Oscar had gotten to know us down in third class where my family... mother, father, my little brother Thaddeus, and I...were kept. I say kept, because it was more like a prison than anything I have known or will ever know. The British will insist on their class system until time will no longer endure it. Back then, no one even questioned it. Oscar said that my brother and I reminded him of his own two sons who were taken away from him by their mother. We said she must be very evil indeed, but he said, no, but warned us of being influenced by relatives.

For the brief duration of the voyage, he played with us and told us fairy stories. He got us laughing so, and our parents as well, that we expressed the hope that the crossing would never end. But of course, too soon, it did.

No one knew who he really was, of course. He said his name was Francis Canterville, and that he was going to America to act the part of a sheriff in Buffalo Bill's Wild West Show. We believed every bit of it, too. At nights, he put on a fancy suit and a false mustache and slipped up to the First Class promenades. I don't know how he did it, but I suspect he charmed the sailors who were on guard against such shenanigans, just as he charmed us.

Well, the fateful night came upon us, the iceberg struck, and no one was down below to help us or tell us what was happening. We boys had been wakened by the terrible jolt and the wrenching sound as we scraped alongside the iceberg. We woke our parents but they said it was nothing to worry about and to go back to sleep, which they did and we didn't. We went out into the passageway and were soon pushed along, far from our bunks, by a frightened crowd of people in their nightclothes. We never saw our parents again. It was bedlam. We were locked in to the lower decks, now filling with water. At one point we heard gunfire.

My little brother was crying and pulling at me, wanting to go find Mama and Papa. It was a pathetic scene, I tell you, and just as I thought we would surely die among strangers, Francis Canterville appeared.

He had fought his way below decks in his first class clothes, just to find the two of us.

"Where are your parents?" he shouted over the din, but we didn't know, and were crying too hard to say if we did. "Come along, now," he commanded. "We will find your parents later. For the present you must be very brave and do everything that I tell you. Now dry your tears, for there is more than enough salt water about than is good for us already."

I think we would have gone to the moon with Francis Canterville. There was no moon that night. The lifeboats were dropping fast as we arrived on the upper deck. We had gotten there by ways that no one but Francis could have thought of, up and around the decks and ladders. He carried us both for part of the way, one under each arm, like two sacks of potatoes. The lifeboat we came to was almost down to the water when we got there. Francis said to me, "You must be a heroic little lad now, Harlan, and wait here while I take your brother down to the boat. I'll be back for you, I promise." Clutching my brother, he grabbed the ropes and slid down to a height where he could safely drop him into the waiting arms of the women below. Then up he came as he had promised, hand over hand, until he was even with me. "Onto my back now," he ordered. "Hang on around my neck." And down we went.

As we came down the rope, he spoke urgently to me. I shall never forget the sound of his voice, commanding and desperate all at once.

I was, of course, scared nearly out of my wits, and what he was saying made no sense to me at the time. It was hours later in the boat, with my brother asleep and I emerging from shock that I understood him. I tried then to engrave what he had said on my mind. These, I believe, are his exact words as we slid down through the icy air over the rocking lifeboat:

"There is a manuscript, hidden in a wall in the Palazzo Contarini in Venice, Italy. When you are grown find this book and make it known. Do this for me, as I have done this for you." And with that he kissed the top of my head and released me into the boat. The women cried for him to leap in with them, but he could see that there was no more room, and instead made his way back up the rope to the doomed vessel.

Oh what a sight that ship was from the lifeboat! We rowed rapidly away. I think everyone in the boat was crying except myself. I was staring hard, trying to make out Francis on the deck but, large as he was, I couldn't see him. I looked for my parents, too, but they were probably still below decks, and I hoped still fast asleep, though I knew better. I have always wished that somehow they knew we were saved before they met their end.

Suddenly, the mighty ship heaved to one end, and the lights went out. A great wail of grief and fear went up from those still on board and those in the boats. The band, which was playing "Nearer my God to Thee," ceased to play, men and instruments tumbling along the decks. We watched while the ship slid, like a sleek seal, beneath the waters. Momentarily all was silent. Then we began to make out the cries of those, less fortunate than ourselves, who had jumped from the ship or been carried back up to the surface by the currents. They were in the water and crying for help as we were rowed farther and farther away into the night.

I suppose you can put together the rest. When I was in Italy between the great wars, I did as Francis had requested of me, and was granted permission to search the palazzo. I found the manuscript, much damaged by dampness. Over the years I have bought, borrowed and begged the other papers and letters that help fill out the story. I have made it a life's work, a mission—to put as much of his story together as I could.

There, now you have it all. I know you will be sure that it sees the light of day.

If God is Time, then the remembrance of things past is prayer.

With kind regards and best wishes,
HARLAN GILL

P.S. I enclose a letter forwarded to me by the second cousin of Timothy Tyharde, found among his belongings in an attic in Drumwillig. It is the last, but certainly not least, chapter in our story. And comes to us in Oscar's own words.

R.M.S. TITANIC
February 12, 1912

My Dearest Tim…

You shall have your note in a bottle describing life aboard ship. I shall fling it into the sea as the vessel makes its final plunge. By the time it washes ashore and makes its way from some discovering hand along an unknown strand to you in Drumwillig, you will know much more about what happened to this great ship on this grim night than I do. Evidently an iceberg has outwitted all of British navigation and engineering. One refrains from comment.

It is all terror now for those left on board, those who are afraid to die, which may be all but myself. The Gypsy said: "fear death by water." For once, I do not take her advice. I feel no fear at all, only a sense of pleasant irony regarding myself, and deep sadness for all the others, be they in silks or homespun. We will all die as one class.

I once expressed disappointment in the Atlantic Ocean.

Could it be seeking its revenge?

So I am to die at last, but having lived the strangest life that ever there was. Thank you for the precious additional years you gave me, each lived as a gift beyond measure, each a pearl of great price. Thank you, thank you, dearest Tim. I must, like Christ, descend for a time to the depths, but soon—perhaps by the time that you read this missive— Eleanora and I will be smiling down upon you from on high and dry. (I, from a great, poofy cloud.) If you feel a sudden urge to cast off your respectability and leave Scotland for Morocco that will be me meddling in the service of your happiness, once again.

I sit now in the first class dining saloon on the artful wallpaper, now turned to the angle of a sloping hillside. This time the wallpaper and I will go together. I am drinking the very best of the champagne on board. Another bottle stands empty, awaiting this note, a cork, some candle wax, and a thrilling plunge into the icy seas. I have never been more sober. I have never been so at peace.

I am afraid the good citizens of Wyoming will have to wait for their Shakespeare. My ideas tend to be about a century ahead of their time, so it will be a long while before another visionary walks among the good citizens of that much ignored state, bringing Romeo and Mercutio as his companions.

Delmonico's, too, will be poorer for the loss of me. In what was to be my newest pose—Frank O'Cantor, newly arrived immigrant from Irish aristocracy (that is not an oxymoron)—I had planned to cut a fine figure of fashion and make astonishing conversation over beefsteak and beer. I wonder what other talents, besides my own, will soon disappear beneath the waves tonight.

Timothy, do me a great favor. There are two small boys by the names of Thaddeus and Harlan Gill who will, God willing, survive this dreadful night. They drift away in a lifeboat as I write. I have told their parents of their rescue, and I hope it brings them some comfort in the dire moments yet to come. See to them, Tim. Be sure they find their relations in England or America. Be sure there is money to care for them. Much is left in my account from Eleanora, and little Alfred will not require so much, coddled as he is by the Parisian contingent. Look after these orphaned children as Robbie Ross has looked after mine, and as I have looked after Eleanora's. They are not mine, they are not yours, but all children are the children of all.

The ship has taken what I sense to be its penultimate lurch; the band plays no more, cries are heard from every direction; the sea pours into the dining saloon through the portholes and the doors. I have scrambled up onto a floating table, the water rises all around me. China plates and cups float about in confusion. I shall not need to hurl the champagne bottle with this message to you into the sea; I need only to extend my arm and let my wrist go limp.

Here then are my last words sent across time—from my present into yours. God bless you. Have Patience in all things. I am glad to be rid of her. I only betrayed our precious secret once in all these years…just before leaving Venice I sent a photograph of myself purloined from Aveline Tartine to Bosie Douglas.

Nothing came of it. Forgive me, for I couldn't help myself. Love to Charles. Tell him I remember what was in the parcel. Prudence implores me to swim. Adieu.

OSCAR

P.S. Do not be sad, dear Tim. Remember that it was I who penned the lines:

> "For he who lives more lives than one
> More deaths than one must die."

ACKNOWLEDGMENTS

For several years after Oscar Wilde died in the humble rooms of the Hôtel d'Alsace in Paris, a group of his devotees would meet there and wonder where he was hiding. They could not accept that such an extraordinary presence was gone from their world forever. This band of true believers inspired the writing of this novel.

Another band of believers have aided and abetted this enterprise, among them Ann Davies, Carol Waldman, Michael, Meredith and Daniel Bergmann, Bruna Nardelli, and the late Richard Olney and Cristiana Fusco. And, most recent thanks to Ulrich Baer and Mary Bahr for giving Oscar yet another life.

They are acknowledged with deep appreciation.

ABOUT THE AUTHOR

Ardythe Ashley is the author of the novels *The Christ of the Butterflies* and *In The Country of the Great King.* While researching *The Return of the Century* she found herself in the Library of the British Museum reading the letters Oscar Wilde wrote in his dank cell in Reading Gaol to Lord Alfred Douglas (Bosie), later published as *De Profundis.* "I'm sorry, Madam," came the firm-but-not-unkind voice of a white-gloved librarian, "but it is not permitted to weep upon the manuscripts." In addition to being a writer, Ashley is a retired psychoanalyst and forever a New Yorker (at heart).

OTHER BOOKS BY OSCAR WILDE
AVAILABLE FROM WARBLER PRESS

The Picture of Dorian Gray

The Importance of Being Earnest

An Ideal Husband

Lady Windermere's Fan

*My Own Dear Darling Boy: The Letters of Oscar Wilde
to Lord Alfred Douglas*

Wilde on Love (part of the
Warbler Press *Contemplations* series)

warblerpress.com